PR

DON
best-sellii

C000115784

"Time travel, ancient legends, and seductive romance are seamlessly interwoven into one captivating package."

—Publishers Weekly on Midnight's Master

"Dark, sexy, magical. When I want to indulge in a sizzling fantasy adventure, I read Donna Grant."

—Allison Brennan, New York Times bestseller

5 Stars! Top Pick! "An absolute must read! From beginning to end, it's an incredible ride."

—Night Owl Reviews

"It's good vs. evil Druid in the next installment of Grant's Dark Warrior series. The stakes get higher as discerning one's true loyalties become harder. Grant's compelling characters and continued presence of previous protagonists are key reasons why these books are so gripping. Another exciting and thrilling chapter!"

—RT Book Reviews on Midnight's Lover

"I definitely recommend Dangerous Highlander, even to skeptics of paranormal romance – you just may fall in love with the MacLeods."

—The Romance Reader

Don't miss these other spellbinding novels by
DONNA GRANT

LaRue Series

Moon Kissed

Chiasson Series

Wild Fever
Wild Dream
Wild Need

Rogues of Scotland Series

The Craving
The Hunger

Dark King Series

Dark Heat
Darkest Flame
Fire Rising
Burning Desire

Dark Warrior series

Midnight's Master
Midnight's Lover
Midnight's Seduction
Midnight's Warrior
Midnight's Kiss
Midnight's Captive
Midnight's Temptation
Midnight's Promise
Midnight's Surrender

DARK SWORD SERIES

Dangerous Highlander
Forbidden Highlander
Wicked Highlander
Untamed Highlander
Shadow Highlander
Darkest Highlander

SHIELD SERIES

A Dark Guardian
A Kind of Magic
A Dark Seduction
A Forbidden Temptation
A Warrior's Heart

DRUIDS GLEN SERIES

Highland Mist
Highland Nights
Highland Dawn
Highland Fires
Highland Magic
Dragonfyre

SISTERS OF MAGIC TRILOGY

Shadow Magic
Echoes of Magic
Dangerous Magic

Royal Chronicles Novella Series

Prince of Desire
Prince of Seduction
Prince of Love
Prince of Passion

**And look for more anticipated novels from
Donna Grant**

Hot Blooded (Dark Kings)
*The Tempted (*Rogues of Scotland*)*
Moon Thrall (LaRue)

coming soon!

MOON KISSED

A LaRue Story

DONNA GRANT

This is a work of fiction. All of the characters, organizations, and events portrayed in this novel are either products of the author's imagination or are used fictitiously.

Moon Kissed

www.DonnaGrant.com

Available in ebook and print editions

PRONUNCIATIONS &
GLOSSARY

GLOSSARY:

Andouille (ahn-doo-ee) & **Boudin** (boo-dan)
Two types of Cajun sausage. Andouille is made with pork while boudin with pork and rice.

Bayou (by-you)
A sluggish stream bigger than a creek and smaller than a river

Beignet (bin-yay)
A fritter or doughnut without a hole, sprinkled with powdered sugar

Cajun ('ka-jun)
A person of French-Canadian descent born or living along southern Louisiana.

Etoufee (ay-two-fay)
Tangy tomato-based sauce dish usually made with crawfish or shrimp and rice

Gumbo (gum-bo)
Thick, savory soup with chicken, seafood, sausage, or wild game

Hoodoo (hu-du)

Also known as "conjure" or witchcraft. Thought of as "folk magic" and "superstition". Some say it is the main force against the use of Voodoo.

Jambalaya (jom-bah-LIE-yah)
Highly seasoned mixture of sausage, chicken, or seafood and vegetables, simmered with rice until liquid is absorbed

Maman (muh-mahn)
Term used for grandmother

Parish
A Louisiana state district; equivalent to the word county

Sha (a as in cat)
Term of affection meaning darling, dear, or sweetheart.

Voodoo (vu-du) – New Orleans
Spiritual folkways originating in the Caribbean. New Orleans Voodoo is separate from other forms (Haitian Vodou and southern Hoodoo). New Orleans Voodoo puts emphasis on Voodoo Queens and Voodoo dolls.

Zydeco (zy-dey-coh)
Accordion-based music originating in Louisiana combined with guitar and violin while combing traditional French melodies with Caribbean and blues influences

PRONUNCIATION:

Arcineaux (are-cen-o)

Chiasson (ch-ay-son)

Davena (dav-E-na)

Delia (d-ee-l-ee-uh)

Delphine (d-eh-l-FEEN)

Dumas (dOO-mah-s)

Gilbeaux (g-ih-l-b-oh)

Lafayette (lah-fai-EHt)

LaRue (l-er-OO)

ACKNOWLEDGEMENTS

A special thanks goes out to my family who lives in the bayous of Louisiana. Those summers there are some of my best memories. I also need to send a shout-out to my team – Bridgette B, Candace C, Stephanie D, Kelly M, Kristin N, Vanessa R, Shani S. You guys are the bomb. Hats off to my editor, Chelle Olson, and design extraordinaire, Leah Suttle. Thank you all for helping me get this story out!

Lots of love to my amazing family. Thanks for putting up with my hectic schedule and for knowing when it was time that I got out of the house. And a special hug for my furbabies Lexi, Sheba, Sassy, Tinkerbell, and Diego.

Last but not least, my readers. You have my eternal gratitude for the amazing support you show me and my books. Y'all rock my world. Stay tuned at the end of this story for the first sneak peek of *Hot Blooded*, Dark Kings book 4 out December 30, 2014. Enjoy!

Xoxo
Donna

CHAPTER ONE

Gator Bait Bar
New Orleans, Louisiana

Myles looked through the receipts from the night before from his seat at the end of the bar. While he tallied their profits and balanced the books, his younger brother, Kane, was going through their liquor supply to place another order.

A shout from the pool tables interrupted Myles as he was inputting numbers in his laptop. He turned his head to the side and glared at his other two brothers – Solomon and Court – who were enjoying their daily pool game, making it difficult for him to do his duty as their CPA.

The games began when Court was barely tall enough to play properly. Solomon was the one to teach Court the game, beating him soundly every time. It was a LaRue trait that once they set their minds to something, they didn't relent until they had whatever it was they wanted. For Court, that had been beating

Solomon. When it had finally happened, Solomon had been unprepared, thinking he still had years of winning ahead of him.

From that day onward, there had been few things that disrupted their daily games, and that included hurricanes.

"You'd think they would've ended the rivalry," Kane said without looking up from his clipboard as he wrote down numbers.

Myles watched his brother closely. After the fiasco with the daughter of the Devil himself, Delphine, and their cousins in Lyons Point, Kane hadn't been the same.

Then again, who would be unchanged after being cursed by a Voodoo priestess out to annihilate your family?

"They'll be using walkers and still playing pool," Myles said. He closed his laptop. Kane was tense, too tense. "You know, you'll have to talk about what happened one day."

Kane was in the process of replacing a bottle of Ciroc vodka on the shelf when he froze. There was the slightest tightening of his shoulders before he turned his head and glowered at Myles with his bright blue eyes – eyes that every LaRue had.

"I've done all the talking I'm going to," Kane stated in a hard voice.

Myles didn't respond as Kane turned back around. Everything about Kane was perfectly tailored, from his golden blond hair to his shirt tucked into his jeans down to the laces of his shoes exactly the same size when tied. This was not the Kane of old. That Kane would roll out of bed with his messy hair, throw on a tee shirt and jeans, and flash a smile that stopped women in their tracks.

This new Kane was too uptight, too...controlled.

"It's not your fault."

Kane whirled around, his eyes blazing with fury, but there was no shouting from this new Kane. His nostrils flared, his hands fisted. "It's my fault I caught Delphine's attention. Wasn't it bad enough that one of our ancestors screwed with a Voodoo priestess and caused us to be werewolves? Apparently, not for me. I thought I could do whatever I wanted. Delphine wanted to teach me a lesson." Kane snorted derisively. "She wanted Ava killed, and who better to do it than the cousin of the Chiassons who were protecting her?"

"You didn't kill her," Myles pointed out.

Kane rolled his eyes. "It's a good thing too, or Lincoln would've skinned me. And I would've welcomed it. We know what we are, who we are when we shift, but if I had killed Ava, all of my memories would've been wiped. I'd have been a monster. Just like those we hunt."

"It's why we called our cousins, remember? We couldn't come after you because we'd captured Delphine." Myles always wanted to scrub himself in acid after he thought of that vile bitch. It had taken almost every trick they knew to confine Delphine, and then it nearly backfired on them.

Kane braced his hands on the bar and let out a deep breath. "I was reckless, Myles. I didn't just put our family at risk, I put our cousins', as well. If Ava hadn't been with them..." he trailed off, unable to answer.

It was a feeling each of them experienced. Kane was dealing with nearly losing himself to the wolf within, but he had no idea how the events had changed the rest of them. And Myles wasn't about to tell him.

It hadn't been just the curse from Delphine or even capturing her, it was Court sprinkling the goofer dust around them so none of Delphine's people could get to her. It was Solomon ready to kill every last one of her followers. It was Myles with his fangs around Delphine's throat, ready to clamp down.

That night, all three of the brothers had been prepared – and willing – to do anything and everything to save Kane.

"It'd been too long since we saw the Chiassons. Both sides of the family have been so busy fighting the supernatural that, we forgot each other." Myles shrugged with a grin, hoping to take both of their minds off Delphine. "You changed all that."

Kane shot him a look and tossed a towel at him. The softening of Kane's mouth was as close to a smile as they would get, but it was enough for Myles.

Since it wasn't yet ten in the morning, all four LaRues were surprised when the door to the bar opened and a woman with hair so brown it was almost black walked in. She shoved the long hair over her shoulder as the door shut behind her and looked around the room with bright blue eyes.

Myles slid off the stool as he realized he was looking at his only female cousin, Riley Chiasson. He stopped in front of her and smiled. "The last time I saw you, you were in pigtails and running roughshod over your brothers."

Riley's smile was slow, showing a dimple in her left cheek. "I wondered if you'd know who I was."

"With eyes like that?" Solomon said as he set down his cue stick atop the pool table and walked to her. "There's no denying our family. What brings you to our neck of the woods?"

Riley swallowed and looked at each of them until she met Myles' gaze. "Since you so graciously pointed out that I was a little girl the last time we saw each other, names put to faces would be great."

Myles pointed to Solomon. "That's the jackass who thinks just because he's the eldest, he can make decisions for us."

"Solomon," Riley said with a nod at him.

"Next up in the order is me," Myles said, waiting to see if she would know.

Riley raised a dark brow. "Then you're Myles."

"Very good," he said. "The scowling one behind the bar is next."

Riley's smile slipped as she shifted her gaze. "Kane." They stared at each other for a heartbeat before Riley turned her head to the pool table. "Which leaves the youngest, Court."

Solomon crossed his arms over his chest. "Now that that's settled, why not tell us why you're visiting."

When she hesitated, Myles wrapped an arm around her and walked her to the bar where Kane filled a glass with ice and then water. She sat on one of the stools and closed her fingers around the glass.

Myles exchanged a look with Solomon. By the way Riley was acting, it was obvious she hadn't told her brothers where she was.

"Do you know I was sent away?" she asked, her gaze on the bar. "Vin said he didn't want me to be a part of the family business."

"You're his only sister. I'd have done the same," Court said as he joined them.

Riley shrugged. "I'd have liked to have some say in it. All of my brothers agreed with Vin, even Beau. The day after I graduated high school, Vincent drove me to

Austin. I've lived in Texas for years. Going to college, working. I wanted to go home."

"Did you tell Vin that?" Solomon asked.

Riley shook her head. "I thought it would be okay to go home since Vin was marrying Olivia, and Lincoln and Ava were together."

"You just showed up, didn't you?" Kane asked softly.

Riley looked up at him. "Olivia and Ava knew what I had planned. They told me how Beau had met Davena. There were three women at the house now. I figured that meant Vin wouldn't keep me away."

"But you didn't know about everything that'd happened," Myles guessed.

Riley snorted and said, "The Chiassons and LaRues have been fighting the supernatural since before I was born. My mother had five children and still fought beside her husband. I should be able to go home."

"Your brothers just want what's best." Solomon took the stool on her left. "Surely you understand that."

"I do, but I haven't seen my home in over four years. They always seemed to have some crisis or another around my breaks that prevented me from returning."

Myles saw the desolation and unhappiness in her gaze, a look he recognized all too well in Kane's eyes of late. "So what happened when you showed up?"

"There was no big, happy family reunion as I'd hoped," she said with a laugh, her lips in a tight smile. "Vin was furious. He and Olivia got in a huge fight because she tried to convince him to let me stay. It didn't take long for all of them to begin arguing. That's when Vin told me to go back to Texas. I told him to kiss my ass and I stormed out to my car. Then I started driving. Before I knew it, I was here."

Court leaned his forearms on the end of the bar. "I spoke to Christian yesterday. He filled me in on Delphine's appearance in Lyons Point. These are dangerous times, Riley."

"They're always dangerous. Riley's a Chiasson. She knows how to fight," Kane said to Court. He then turned his gaze to Riley. "What's your plan?"

She tucked her hair behind her ear. "I'd like to stay here a couple of days to figure out what I'll do next. If that's okay."

"Next?" Solomon repeated. "You're not going back to Austin?"

Her smile was sad. "I graduated in June. My brothers don't even know. All the times I called home, they didn't have time to talk because of something they were hunting. I had no family in attendance. I even remained for a few months thinking they might realize their mistake, but there's always something to keep them from remembering me."

Kane covered her hand with his. "They remember. Trust me. You had a chance at a normal life, Riley. They didn't. Neither did we."

"Of course," she said too quickly.

Myles wasn't fooled. Riley was hurting, and she needed someplace to lick her wounds. "You're welcome here for as long as you need."

His brothers were nodding in agreement before he finished talking.

"Thank you, but I can only accept on one condition," Riley said.

Court shrugged, not understanding. "Name it."

"None of you can tell any of my brothers or their women."

Riley might be beautiful, but she had a sharp mind. At that moment, Myles realized the trap she'd led them into. If they didn't allow her to stay, they couldn't keep an eye on her, and as hunters—and her family—that was their duty. By making them agree to her terms, she ensured that she wouldn't have her brothers descending upon her to get her back to Texas.

"I never saw that coming," Kane said, one side of his lips lifted in a grin.

Myles caught Solomon's and Court's gaze. Perhaps Riley was just what Kane needed to help him remember to smile and laugh again. Kane could look out for her, which would help him heal.

"You do know the full moon will be here in a few days?" Solomon asked her.

Riley looked at him as if he were a simpleton. "I'm a Chiasson. Of course, I know. So don't bother trying to lecture me. I know the divides in New Orleans where vampires, witches, demons, werewolves, and djinn are housed. I also know enough to stay away from Delphine and anything to do with Voodoo."

"She's a Chiasson, all right," Myles said with a grin.

Riley was a breath of fresh air and seemed to be just what the LaRues needed. Vincent might lament having a sister because of the worry it took to keep her safe, but Myles wondered how different the LaRues' lives would've been if they'd had a sister among them.

"I'll get her settled," Kane said as he came around the bar.

Myles, Solomon, and Court watched the two of them walk from the building with Riley talking and Kane nodding his head.

"I don't know if this is a good idea," Solomon said.

Court ran his hand through his chin-length

butterscotch blond hair. "It's done now. She knew we couldn't let her leave."

"She got Kane to smile. That's a vast improvement over the last few weeks," Myles pointed out. "He needs something to do, and Riley just gave him the opportunity."

Solomon slid off the stool. "Let's hope you're right, because when Vin discovers Riley is here, we may well have the entire Chiasson clan on our asses."

"Think how we could clear out New Orleans with all of us," Court said. "No more pacts with the five houses. New Orleans could be clear once more."

Myles knew Court had been joking, but it made sense. "We can't bring Delphine and her followers down by ourselves. With four more, we'd stand a really good chance."

"Especially with Beau's woman being a witch," Court pointed out.

Solomon pinned Myles with a look. "First, we make sure nothing happens to Riley, because Chiasson or not, she's not been hunting like we have. If anything happens to her—"

"You don't even need to say it," Myles said.

Maybe it wasn't such a good idea that Riley was there.

CHAPTER TWO

Addison Moore sat in her parked car and stared unseeing out of the windshield. In her hands was a letter that had changed her life in a second.

Something dropped onto the paper. Addison looked down and saw the bead of wetness that soaked into the letter. It took her a moment to realize it was the sweat running down her face from being in the car with the engine turned off in hundred-degree heat.

She folded the letter up neatly and tucked it into her purse. Then she opened the door to the car and stepped out into the sunshine.

Addison shut the door and leaned back against the car staring at all the tourists. They were laughing and smiling, not a care in the world. It was so at odds with what she was going through, that it almost felt like she wasn't in her body. That she was on the outside looking in.

"Miss, are you all right?"

Addison shook herself and saw the police officer standing beside her. He was middle-aged, with gray at the temples of his black hair and concern in his eyes.

"Are you lost?" he asked.

She forced a smile. "Just daydreaming, officer. I'm fine."

"You need to get out of the heat and get some water soon," he warned before moving on.

Knowing he was right, Addison pushed away from the car. She hadn't taken two steps before her cell phone buzzed with a text. She reached in her purse for it and then groaned when she saw the text was from her roommate, Wendy.

"I haven't been gone that long," she mumbled as she hastily wrote that she'd have Wendy's car back within the hour.

How she hated not having money for her own vehicle. After only one semester at Tulane, Addison had no choice but to sell her clunker of a car to make ends meet. It had been her only choice, but it also put a heavy strain on her.

Addison put the phone away and strolled along the street. Since the first time she saw New Orleans at the age of ten, she had been fascinated. The history of the city was mesmerizing. The food and vibrancy of the streets and buildings drew a constant crowd no matter the time of year.

Yet there was no denying the dark, dangerous edge of the city either.

Addison walked the streets of the Quarter, watching others stand for pictures or stare in wide-eyed wonder at the cemeteries. By getting a glimpse into someone else's life, she was able to forget hers for a short while.

A glance at her watch proved that her hour was almost up. Reluctantly, she started back to the car. She wasn't ready to return to the university, not when it was the end of her time there.

"Stop pitying yourself," she said aloud. "Stand tall. Stand proud. You're a Moore."

Those were the last words her father had said before he was deployed. He was a career Navy man, never happy unless he was at sea. That never bothered her because he always came home. Until he hadn't.

Addison didn't want to think about her father, or the lonely years after. At twenty-three, she was ready to get on with her life, except that she couldn't do that until she finished her degree.

Which was going to be impossible now that the last of her scholarship had run out. Her student loans were reaching cosmic proportions already. If she were lucky, she might pay them off before she died.

She was almost to the car when a scream rent the air. Someone came rushing toward her, knocking her to the ground. Addison looked up in time to see a young kid with a navy hoodie duck into an alley.

Suddenly, people began to crowd around. Someone helped her to her feet as sirens blared. Addison looked down to see that both knees were scraped and bleeding, and her shirt was ripped.

"Excuse me. Pardon me," she said as she slowly made her way through the throng of people to the car.

She reached the car and glanced around to see someone pointing her out to a policeman. Addison stilled and waited for the officer to reach her. It was the same one from earlier.

"Did you see what happened?" he asked.

She threw up her hands. "I've no idea what happened. I heard a scream, then someone ran into me and knocked me down."

"Do you remember anything about the person?"

"I saw what looked like a teenager with a hoodie duck into the alley."

The policeman's face was grim. "I'm going to need a formal statement from you."

"Because the guy bumped into me?" she asked in disbelief

"Because he mugged an elderly woman. When he took her purse, she fell and hit her head. She's dead."

Addison briefly squeezed her eyes closed. "Oh, my God. I had no idea."

In seconds, she was taken to a patrol car and driven to the station. She sat there for the next hour waiting on someone to take her statement while her phone blew up with texts from an angry Wendy. Another hour passed while she wrote everything down and went over it with another officer before she was driven back to Wendy's car.

Addison stared at the spot where the red Miata was supposed to be parked, to find a gray Dodge truck instead. She was about to try and catch the police before they left when she remembered telling Wendy where she'd parked the car in one of the dozens of texts they'd exchanged.

Anger spiked through her as she punched Wendy's number and listened while the phone rang. It took three rings before Wendy answered. "Do you have the car?" Addison asked.

"Yeah. I had Paul drop me off," Wendy said with music from the radio blaring in the background. "I told you, I have to be at my parent's tonight by eight. I couldn't wait."

"I wish you'd have told me you picked up the car. I thought it was stolen."

Wendy laughed. "Nope. I've got it. Gotta go! I'll see

you Monday."

Addison looked at the phone after Wendy ended the call. It had never entered Wendy's mind that Addison didn't have a way back to the apartment they shared.

Her stomach rumbled. She had skipped lunch because there hadn't been time between her classes, and now she felt as if she could eat her own arm she was so hungry. With only five dollars to her name, she could either eat or take the bus home. Since there was nothing to eat at the apartment, her choice was made for her.

Addison looked first one way and then the other. She turned left and strolled down the street looking for a place she thought she could afford. There was about a hundred dollars left to charge on her lone credit card. She had been saving that for something special like books, but food was a lot more important.

She heard the music before she saw the place. While many of the restaurants played Zydeco music, there was a bar on the corner of the street blaring Theory of a Deadman. The song was Drown, her favorite.

Addison smiled when she looked up at the sign of the bar swinging above her. It was a wooden sign made to look as if a huge bite had been taken out of one corner of the top. Painted on the sign was an alligator with its mouth open.

"Gator Bait," Addison read the sign aloud. "Fitting."

She stepped into the bar and was immediately taken in by the atmosphere. The wood floor had seen many shoes, but the bar to her left was so polished it shone. On the walls were hundreds of pictures of famous people who had visited the place, as well as a few well-placed jaws from dead alligators. The music was loud, the patrons drinking, eating, and having a good time.

Addison walked to the bar and took a seat on a black barstool. She spotted the laminated menu just out of reach down the bar. Leaning over, she managed to grab it without bumping the guy's beer next to her.

There wasn't a lot on the menu, but it all looked good, and the prices were reasonable enough that she might even give in to temptation and order a drink. After the day she'd had, she needed it.

"Can I help you?"

She glanced up from the menu with a smile and was startled by the bright blue gaze of the guy behind the bar. "Yeah, I think I'd like to try a bowl of the red beans and rice with cornbread, please."

"One of our specialties," he replied with a grin. "What can I get you to drink?"

A quick glance at their drinks and one caught her eye. "I'd like to try the Devil's Bribe."

He grinned at her choice. "I'll be right back."

She watched him walk away, noticing that he was good-looking with his blond hair and blue eyes. Addison set aside the menu and realized the guy on her left was staring.

"Can I buy you a drink?" he asked as he looked her over, lust in his hazel eyes. His bushy brown beard was long and looked to have food in it left over from lunch, making her stomach roll. A yellow bandana was tied around his forehead, and he wore a tee shirt pulled tight over his beer belly.

She clutched her purse in her lap. "Thank you, but I've already ordered."

"I can get the next one. Let me treat you."

"I think I'll pass." She looked around, hoping there

was another place to sit because the guy was making her uncomfortable.

He burped loudly, then leaned close. "You think you're better than me?"

"No, I…" she began.

"The darts are open, Ed," a deep, sexy voice interrupted her.

Addison's gaze jerked to the source. The new guy stood behind the bar. He was tall and imposing, his ash blond hair so thick looking that she wanted to run her fingers through it. His eyes were so bright a blue they seemed to be lit from within. With his gaze directed at Ed, she got to look her fill.

His face was lean, rugged with a look that bordered on feral. With a clean-shaven jaw, she spotted the muscle that twitched. His lips were sinfully full, too full for such a handsome man, but it made him sexier – if that were possible.

Her eyes dipped to his chest where his shirt looked to be made specifically for him. It hugged his wide shoulders, then tapered down the V of his abdomen to hang just below his hips. The front part of the white shirt was tucked into the waist of his low-slung, dark denim.

When Ed moved off to the darts, the man drew in a deep breath, stretching the white shirt and the dark blue stitching. Her gaze lifted back to his face, and this time, his startling blue eyes were directed at her.

Addison's breath locked in her lungs as if the air had been sucked from the room. She could only stare, her voice deserting her. She was struck senseless, pulled into his mesmerizing blue gaze.

"I apologize for Ed. He can get a little rowdy when he sees a beautiful woman."

Like an idiot, all Addison could do was nod. She wanted to say something witty or funny, but her mind was completely blank. How was she supposed to put together a coherent thought when such a hunk of a man was looking at her? It's like asking a fly to milk a cow – impossible.

His face relaxed, a hint of a smile playing about his lips. "Have you been helped?"

Again, she nodded.

Dammit, Addison. You could've answered that. You know that answer.

Did she? She was no longer sure.

"I don't think I've seen you around before." He leaned one hand on the bar and she spotted the wide leather cuff around his right wrist. "Is this your first time to Gator Bait?"

"Yes," she said, refusing to nod mutely again.

"A tourist?"

That caused Addison to laugh. "No. I'm usually working or studying. I don't get out much."

"Then I'm glad you aren't doing either tonight."

She could feel the blush creeping up her neck to her cheeks. "Me, too."

"I'm Myles LaRue," he said and stuck out his hand.

Her hand fit into his, warmth seeping from his palm to hers as something sensual and needy spiraled through her at their touch. "Addison Moore."

They stayed like that for a moment, their hands together, their eyes locked. Addison couldn't begin to explain the strangeness of the situation, or how she prayed it would continue.

Someone cleared his throat, and she saw another man come stand beside Myles. Addison tried to pull her hand away, but Myles tightened his grip a fraction, halting her. He winked, making her smile as he released her hand.

"Court seems to have brought your food," Myles said as he took the bowl from Court and placed it in front of her.

"Since you're out here, brother, you can fix her drink. She wanted the Devil's Bribe," Court said as he slapped Myles on the back and turned to leave.

Addison couldn't stop the laughter that bubbled up as Myles popped Court on the leg with the towel as he walked off.

CHAPTER THREE

Myles was utterly charmed by the mysterious, exquisite Addison with her champagne colored chin-length, wavy hair. In the dimness of the bar, he wasn't sure of the exact shade of her eyes, but they were striking in how they held his gaze. There was a hint of coyness along with sincerity that made his balls tighten.

The simple fact that desire burned through his veins should have been enough to send him running as fast and far from her as he could get. Yet he remained, hoping to hear more of her husky voice.

Her skin was dew-kissed, a healthy glow that made him itch to run his hands all over her body. Her sleeveless peach tank dipped low, giving him a tantalizing view of the swells of her breasts.

His hands fisted on the bar. It took a herculean effort to realize that Court was back and talking to him. He shot his brother a look, irritated to have his attention diverted from Addison. Myles returned his gaze to her as she put a bite of the red beans and rice in her mouth.

Her large eyes watched him, but he couldn't make himself stop staring. She had the face of an angel, sweet and sensual. Her mouth was a temptation in itself, with her pouty lips that could have him on his knees in a matter of seconds if she knew her power.

An image flashed in his head of Addison in his arms, her head thrown back as she moaned in pleasure. His cock went instantly, achingly hard.

He was royally fucked.

"Y'all wouldn't by chance be hiring?" Addison asked.

Myles blinked. It took him a few moments for her words to penetrate his fog of desire. He glanced at the women walking around in short denim shorts and tight, black shirts with the Gator Bait logo.

He really couldn't think now. He'd be a puddle of need if he had to see Addison wearing those outfits every day.

"Yes," Court leaned over and said. "We are, actually. I've got an application in the back. When you get finished eating, Myles can take you to his office."

Myles definitely wanted to take her, but it wasn't to his office. He cleared his throat and pushed away from the bar. He had to put some distance between them. "Yes. My office."

Damn. Did he sound as stupid as he thought he did? When Court raised a brow in question while trying not to laugh, Myles had his answer.

With as busy as the bar was, Myles couldn't stand around and talk. He used that excuse to help Court with the drinks since Solomon was in the back cooking, and Kane was still getting Riley settled.

A little while later, Myles looked up again. Addison had her back to him with her elbows resting on the bar as she nodded her head along to the music. Her gaze was on the pool competition that was a weekly event.

Her food had been cleared, and her drink was empty. Beside it was a glass of soda that was also empty. Myles dumped the melting ice and refilled it before pouring her a fresh soda.

He set it down. As he was about to walk away, she turned her head and their eyes met.

She glanced down at the drink. "Thank you."

"Anytime. Do you play pool?"

Her laugh went straight to his still hard cock. "I can get a ball in the hole if I'm lucky, but I'm rarely lucky. I am enjoying the tournament though." She turned around on the stool and took a long drink of the soda. "I heard the guy next to me tell his friend y'all do this weekly, and then have a larger tournament for the weekly winners at the end of the month."

"Yep. We've been playing pool since we could walk. I think the first thing our father put in our hands was a miniature pool stick." Myles smiled at the memory of their parents.

"Your father must have really loved to play."

Myles pulled a frosted mug from the fridge and pulled the lever for a blonde ale, one of their bestselling draft beers. Once the mug was full, he set it in front of the customer. "My mom was pretty good at it herself. When we decided to open the bar, it just seemed natural to put in a couple pool tables."

"So you and Court opened this together?" she asked.

"I have three brothers. Solomon, Kane, and Court. The four of us went in together."

She wrinkled up her nose. "I've heard it's never good to go into business with family."

That was true for most families, but then again, those families weren't cursed to turn into werewolves. "We're a tight family."

"And your parents? Do they approve?"

Court was walking past, and as he heard her question, a glass slipped from his fingers to bounce against the mat and then hit the floor, shattering. "Shit," he mumbled and hurried to clean it up.

Myles started to help his youngest brother, but it took only one furious look from Court to stop him. Their parents were a sore subject, even after so many years. Myles turned back to Addison. "Our parents are dead."

"I'm sorry."

She said it without the embarrassment of discovering death, but with the sincerity of someone well acquainted with it. The more Myles spoke to her, the more he wanted to know.

"Thank you," he mumbled. "It was a long time ago."

"Those wounds never go away."

Now he knew someone close to her had died, and he would bet it was her parents. "No, they don't."

"You're lucky to have siblings to turn to."

The conversation needed some levity. "When I'm not wanting to knock their heads off. Do you have any siblings?"

"It's just me," she replied with a too-bright smile. "So, how long has this place been in business?"

"Ten years or so. Are you sure you want to work here? The tips are good for the girls, but things can get rowdy on occasion."

Addison shrugged. "I need the job."

Kane did the hiring, but Myles knew there was

nothing about Addison that would prevent his brother from bringing her on. "Give me a moment and I'll take you to the office."

"Take your time. I don't have anywhere to be," she said with a smile before turning back to the pool game.

Court stopped beside Myles and said over the music, "You're looking at her as if you want to devour her. I say make your move."

Every time Myles thought about having a relationship, all he had to do was look at Solomon. "We know how those things end."

"If our cousins can do it, so can we?"

"The Chiassons don't have our...affliction," Myles reminded him.

Court glanced at Addison again. "You want her. There's no reason you can't have her, even if it's only for a little while."

"As long as she works here, all I'll ever do is look."

~ ~ ~

Two excruciating days later, Myles was still looking. Just as he expected, Kane hired Addison the night she applied. She started working the next day, and each time she came in wearing the tight black shirt and denim shorts, Myles couldn't think of anything but her.

He tried staying in his office, but that didn't work. He tried remaining in the kitchen so he could only catch glimpses of her, but it wasn't enough. He then tried working behind the bar, which proved too much any time a patron so much as gave her an admiring look.

Nickleback played through the speakers, and Addison swayed with the music as she set up the tables.

"She's pretty," Riley said as she put glasses away, readying for the evening crowd.

Myles glanced at his cousin, knowing none of her brothers would likely approve of her working there. "I suppose."

Riley snorted loudly. "You're a terrible liar, Myles. You've been staring at her for days, and when you aren't looking, she's staring at you."

That was exactly what he didn't want to hear. It made him want to pursue whatever was between them, but it wasn't something any of the LaRues would ever attempt again.

Riley set a glass down and positioned herself so that he had to look at her. "What is it? Are you telling me you won't go after her? Why? My brothers manage it."

"We're not exactly like your brothers."

She rolled her blue eyes and smoothed her hands over her hair pulled back into a sleek ponytail. "Your father and grandfather didn't see an issue. Nor did any of your other ancestors." She frowned suddenly. "Something happened, didn't it? Something to make all of you shy away from relationships."

Myles glanced through the arched doorway to the kitchen where Solomon was. "Leave it, Riley. Please."

"Do my brothers know?"

"No, and we want it to stay that way," he warned her.

She put her hand on his arm. "It must have been pretty bad."

"You can't begin to fathom it."

Riley dropped her hand and swallowed. "Ava said her father is here. I haven't seen him."

"Jack does his own thing. He comes and goes often. There is a lot of hunting to be done around here."

"Hunting?" Addison said as she walked up and placed some dirty glasses on the bar. "What do you hunt?"

Myles had been so lost in the past that he hadn't realized Addison was near. Otherwise, he would've never spoken. "Anything really."

"You know these Cajun boys," Riley said as she turned to face Addison. "They do enjoy their hunting."

Addison looked from Riley to Myles, and then back to Riley, a slight frown marring her forehead. "Right."

Myles didn't let out his breath until Addison disappeared into the kitchen. "Speaking of hunting, I think I'm going to go tonight."

"I'm coming with you," Riley said.

Myles jerked away from her. "The hell you are. It's one thing to have you here and not tell your brothers. It's another thing entirely to take you hunting."

"Do you forget I'm a Chiasson? I've known what's out there since I was old enough to hold a weapon. My parents made sure all of us knew how to hunt – and kill – those things."

"Yes, but when was the last time you hunted?"

"Two weeks ago."

Myles ran a hand down his face, suddenly very happy he didn't have a sister. "Are you kidding?"

"Really?" she asked angrily. "You think I went to Austin and pretended evil didn't exist?"

"Do your brothers know what you were doing?"

She put her hands on her hips. "They might have, had they bothered to visit."

"You're going to drive me to drink, Riley," Myles said and sighed. "I know that stubborn streak within you. We all have it. If we don't take you, you'll go hunting yourself. You can come with me tonight. I heard about a wraith being spotted."

She gave him a wink. "Thanks, cuz."

Riley left Myles and made her way to the kitchen. It didn't take her long to find Addison in the back peeling shrimp. "I thought you worked the front."

Addison glanced at her and shrugged. "I do, but everything is ready, and I hate being idle. So I asked Solomon what I could do to help."

"Did I hear Kane right earlier? Do you have another job, as well?"

Addison rubbed her chin on her shoulder. "I've got three all together, but if I can bring home as much money as I did last night on a regular basis, I think I can drop one."

"Are you Super Woman?" Riley asked with a laugh. "Three jobs, and you're still going for your degree? I'm impressed."

"I'm taking the semester off."

Riley was instantly on alert as she heard the break in Addison's voice. "Sometimes we need that break. The classes will still be there in the spring. I was tempted to quit midway through my third year."

"Where did you get your degree?"

"UT. My brothers sent me to Austin as soon as I got my high school diploma."

Addison shifted her weight from one foot to the other as she leaned her hip against the stainless steel table. "So, you're from New Orleans?"

"I was raised a few hours from here." Riley hid a smile as she realized that Addison was trying to see if she was interested in any of the guys. Riley then decided to ease her mind. "I wanted to spend some time with my cousins. The LaRue boys can be a lot of fun."

Addison's head snapped to her. "Cousins?"

"Cousins," Riley repeated and gave in to the smile. "I'll warn you, they're obstinate as mules. Sometimes we women have to show them what it is they want."

"I don't know," Addison hedged.

Riley leaned close. "Trust me. Go after what you want. Or should I say *who* you want." When Addison simply stared at her like a deer in headlights, Riley bumped her shoulder against Addison's. "You never know what tomorrow will bring."

Addison looked through the doorway into the bar at Myles. "That's so true."

CHAPTER FOUR

Addison yawned as she walked from the coffee shop after splurging on a java chip frappuccino. Every day she thought of Riley's words, but she had yet to make any sort of move on Myles.

She had an hour until she had to be at Gator Bait. It had only been a week, but she'd managed to bring in twice as much money as her other two jobs combined. Holding down three jobs was taking its toll on her, which was why she had opted to quit her cleaning job. She kept her job at the attorney's office because of the hours and their willingness to work around her college courses.

Of course, that wasn't an issue this semester.

Addison walked to a bench across the street and sat. Not even the wonders of the French Quarter could pull her from the funk she fell into every time she thought about finishing college.

If she saved everything she made, she might have enough to cover another semester, but what about the one after that? Thanks to the tips from Gator Bait, she was able to pay Wendy for two months past due rent, as well as the current month.

Getting behind on bills sucked the big one. Addison felt as if she were forever getting caught up. It was one of the reasons she wanted a degree, to get a good job so she could make enough money to support herself.

Ever since her father's death, she felt as if she were fighting for handouts. There hadn't been much family to even consider taking her in, but she felt fortunate that she'd had that and wasn't forced into a foster home.

Looking back, Addison knew her first few years with her grandmother might have been strict and regulated, but at least she was loved. After her grandmother died, she'd briefly lived with her mother's brother and his wife until he'd been diagnosed with cystic fibrosis. Then she went to the only other family that could take her in, her father's brother and his wife. They didn't have any children of their own, and they struggled with money, but she had a home.

Addison got her first job two months shy of her sixteenth birthday just so she wouldn't have to ask them for lunch money. And now to learn the truth about them... She couldn't even think about it. Every time she did, she grew so infuriated that she thought she might explode from the anger it was so fierce.

As she sat drinking her frappuccino, Addison's thoughts turned to Myles. At first she believed the sexual tension between them was her imagination. Over the past week, she found him watching her often. His gaze was direct and...needy. The one thing she wasn't was a take-charge kind of girl. She liked the guy to make the first move, but she was seriously considering going outside of her comfort zone when it came to Myles.

He was dependable, steady, and so damn handsome she wanted to lick his entire body. It was sinful for a man to look so good. Not to mention the havoc it played on her hormones.

Myles seemed like the type of guy to go after a woman he wanted. He had yet to make any perceived moves on her though, which probably meant...he wasn't interested.

"Well, this day just gets better and better," she mumbled to herself as she came to the conclusion.

Addison people watched – one of her favorite pastimes – as she continued to wrestle with her thoughts on Myles. If he rejected her, Addison would never be able to step foot inside the bar again. She'd be mortified.

A breeze ruffled her hair, pulling the strands into her eye. She wiped them away, tucking them behind her ear. That's when she spotted a woman with rich, dark hair blatantly staring at her from across the street near a row of artists and fortune tellers.

Addison raised a brow in question. To her shock, the woman started walking toward her. In a city known for its crazies, Addison sat up straighter, prepared to defend herself if need be.

The woman was tall and slender. She wore a gauzy cream shirt that was cinched at the waist with a brown belt. It was paired with a long, full, red skirt with small beige flowers. Around her head was a scarf of cream with dark brown beads hanging against her forehead.

The woman stopped before Addison, her brown eyes large and tilted slightly at the corners. She had mocha skin that hinted at mixed ancestry. "Your life is in danger."

How did one react to such a statement? Addison frowned as she cocked her head. "From you?"

"Of course not," the woman said impatiently and sat down while covertly looking around. "I know you may not believe me, but I saw you in danger last night."

Addison was beginning to wonder if the woman had escaped a mental institute. "Saw me? I doubt that. I was working all night, and the only thing I'm in danger of there is having beer spilled on me."

The woman let out a long, suffering sigh. "When I say I saw you, I mean that I had a vision. I was doing a reading last night when your face flashed in my mind and I saw it all. A wolf was chasing you."

"Whoa," Addison said and scooted away on the bench. "Hold up a minute. Did you just say a reading? Are you a fortune teller?"

The woman rolled her eyes and motioned with her hands to her outfit. "Bingo. Now, can you get past that so you can hear what else I'm saying?"

"I heard you. Danger. Wolf."

She stared at Addison for a moment before she stuck out her hand. "Let's start over. I'm Minka Verdin. I'm from a long line of fortune tellers descended from gypsies that came here from Romania."

"Addison Moore," she said as she shook Minka's hand. "You're serious."

"As a heart attack. Listen, most of the time I bullshit my way through reading someone's palm. I've had visions since I was six years old, but they were stupid, like an image of a live oak outside of town, or an old rusty car sitting in a yard. There have been three instances in my life where I saw someone's face. Last night, it was yours."

Addison didn't want to believe her, but the truth

shining in her eyes couldn't be ignored. "Let's say I believe you. How did you know I'd be here?"

"My stand is over there," Minka said and pointed across the street in the square. "I've had that same space for five years. I didn't just see the wolf chasing you. I saw you sitting here in that same navy shirt and white shorts. So, I kept a lookout."

Addison had lived in New Orleans most of her life. She knew the things said about the city, and she even witnessed some things that made her want to hide under the covers.

"There are no wolves in New Orleans."

Minka turned her gaze away. "Look around. Tell me what you see."

Addison did as she requested. She turned her head from one side to the other. "I see people returning to their jobs after lunch. I see tourists. I see artists painting. I see musicians. Regular, everyday people."

"Do you know what I see?"

She shifted her eyes to Minka, curious. "What?"

Minka pointed to where her stand was behind the artists. "I see witches." She jerked her chin in the direction behind her. "I see demons." Next, she nodded her head to the left. "I see vampires. Farther down the street...werewolves. And to the right are djinn."

"Right," Addison said with a laugh, thinking Minka was teasing her. Then Addison saw her face and the seriousness in which Minka's dark eyes stared. "You want me to believe I'm surrounded by those things? Besides, everyone knows vampires can't come out during the day."

"Yes, they can. They prefer night, but they can move in the daylight. And yes, I want you to believe the supernatural surrounds you, because it does. It always has. New Orleans is a mecca for such creatures."

"Just New Orleans?"

"No," Minka said sadly. "There are other places the supernatural are drawn to, and there are people who hunt them."

Hunters. Addison remembered what she had overheard between Myles and Riley a few days earlier. "If these...beings...know they're being hunted, why do they remain?"

"Because in New Orleans, they have a sort of truce so that all five factions can remain. And they're being watched. If they step out of line, they are eliminated instantly. It keeps the factions in line for the most part. Besides, there are too many of the supernatural gathered here for the local hunters to wipe out by themselves."

"You know these hunters?"

Minka hesitated for a second before she nodded. "I do. I'm part of the supernatural world because I have gifts, but I'm not a threat like vampires, demons, or other things."

"You left out werewolves. Aren't they dangerous?" Addison asked curiously.

Minka bit her bottom lip a moment. "They can be, but they are also loyal to a fault."

"You said one was chasing me. I'm gathering it isn't loyal to me."

"That's just it," Minka said, her forehead furrowing. "He shouldn't have been chasing you."

That got Addison's attention. "He? You know who it is? Tell me so I can keep my distance."

"That might be difficult."

There was something in Minka's tone that set off warning bells in Addison's head. "Who is he?"

"He's not your enemy. If anything, you're safer near him."

"Safer?" she cried, standing up. "You said he was chasing me."

Minka rose to her feet and very calmly said, "That's what I saw, but that doesn't mean that's what happens."

Addison had about had enough. She crossed her arms over her chest. "Did you, or did you not just come over here and tell me I'm in danger?"

"Yes," Minka answered.

"Did you or did you not tell me a werewolf was chasing me in this vision you saw?"

Minka's lips flattened for a moment. "Yes."

"Then why are you backtracking all of a sudden?"

"Did you not hear what else I said?" Minka asked testily. "I said he shouldn't have been chasing you."

Addison dropped her hands and adjusted the strap of her crossbody purse. "Why?"

"I recognized the wolf."

"And?" Addison urged tightly, her patience at an end.

Minka plopped back down on the bench. "He's one of the good guys."

"A werewolf that's good? Isn't that a contradiction of terms?"

"If you knew him, you'd understand," Minka said. "They're known throughout the Quarter, throughout all of New Orleans. They help keep the factions in line. They would never hurt a human."

"But other werewolves would?"

Minka looked up and nodded. "Some."

"You keep saying 'they'."

Minka shook her head and shoved a stray strand of dark hair out of her face. "Have you met any new people recently?"

"I work at a bar. I meet new people every day."

That got Minka's attention. "What bar?"

"Gator Bait."

Minka jumped to her feet again and took a step back. "Watch yourself, Addison. You're in danger, but I don't know from who."

Addison's jaw dropped when Minka turned and began to walk off. "So that's it? You're going to dump that foretelling in my lap and then just walk away."

Minka's steps halted and she looked back at Addison over her shoulder. "I've never told a stranger any of this before. I couldn't help you anyway."

"And if you have another vision that tells you more? Don't you want a way to contact me?" By her hesitation, Addison knew the answer was a resounding no, but whatever drew Minka to proclaim her vision kept her still.

Finally, Minka nodded. "Yes."

"I live in an apartment off of Rue Parc Fontaine. If I'm not there, you can find me at Gator Bait most nights."

Minka nodded. "Be safe, Addison."

CHAPTER FIVE

Myles knew something was wrong with Addison by the way she jumped at every sound. Ever since she'd walked into the bar that afternoon, she had been skittish and hyper-alert. Almost as if she were waiting for someone to attack her.

As if he would allow that to happen. Not in their bar, and most especially not to her.

"Trouble?" Solomon asked.

Myles shrugged from his place at the doorway to the kitchen. "I don't know. Something has Addison spooked."

"She's in New Orleans. She'd be stupid not to be spooked."

"According to Riley, Addison has lived here her entire life. She's lived this long without an incident. Need I remind you that she was enrolled at Tulane until this semester? You know what happens there."

Solomon grunted and let his gaze wander the patrons. "There's no one here that should cause such a reaction."

Myles raised a brow and looked at his brother. "The full moon is upon us. The entire city goes ape shit during this time."

"That could be what's bothering her."

Myles hoped to hell it wasn't. "I've made excuses for you and Court. It'd be hell if Addison saw you after the nice lie I told."

"Point taken. And you and Kane? When will y'all get out?"

"Soon," Myles said and looked back at Addison.

Solomon let out a sigh. "Just because of the...past...doesn't mean you shouldn't take what you so obviously want. Namely, Addison."

Myles turned and put his back to the wall. "You went through the hell, but we were right there with you, brother. We weren't the ones in love with her, but we loved her. You're more of a moron than I thought if you don't think that affected each of us."

"I know it did." Solomon ran a hand down his face lined with fatigue, his blue eyes troubled. "When I was in Lyons Point, I saw Vincent and Linc with their women. I hated them for being able to hold onto that. If they only knew how easy they had it."

Myles clasped his brother's shoulder and squeezed. "Take your anger out on the fuckers stupid enough to cross the line tonight."

Solomon's eyes flashed with an unholy light from the wolf within. "I'll see you out there."

Myles watched Solomon walk out the back door before he checked on the cooks. There was an inordinate amount of humans in the bar, but that's always how it was on a night with a full moon. Humans were temptation to the supernatural that lived in the darkness.

He walked out of the back and gave a nod to Kane, who slipped out without anyone noticing. Myles walked behind the bar where Riley was busy pouring drinks.

"What are you still doing here?" she asked as she glanced at her watch. "The sun just set. You should be out there."

"I'm going. Are you sure you have everything?"

She laughed and popped the caps off two beers with an opener before setting the bottles in front of the customers. "Of course."

Myles leaned close when she turned to run the credit card. "One of us will be close. We never leave the bar completely unattended."

"It'll be fine," she assured him. "Didn't I prove in the last two nights that I know exactly what I'm doing? I took down that wraith, and just last night, two vampires. All by myself. Remember?"

"I remember." He shook his head, unable to hold back a grin. "It's the only reason we aren't locking you in the walk-in fridge in the back."

Riley cut him a dry look. "Very funny. Now get going while Addison is busy."

Myles glanced in Addison's direction to see her taking down an order. Something nagged at him to stay, but he had a job to do. He walked to the kitchen and out the back door to the alley.

He took a quick look to make sure no one was around before he ran two steps, jumped on a stack of crates, and then launched himself over the wooden fence to the roof of the next building.

The moon beckoned, summoned. And the wolf within answered.

~ ~ ~

Addison delivered the fried alligator, dubbed Gator Bites, along with a pitcher of beer to the table of three college guys who eyed her appreciatively. A week ago, she'd have blushed at their blatant looks, but it hadn't taken her long to get used to such things. If she were honest with herself, she would admit that the only one who could make her blush now was Myles.

She turned from the table and looked around for him. At least one of the four LaRue brothers was always at the bar. As far as she could tell, none of them was there now.

Addison decided not to read too much into it. Everyone needed a night off. Hers was supposed to be tomorrow night, but she'd picked up a shift from another waitress who wanted the time off.

She couldn't believe she hadn't thought to get a job at a bar before. She made more money than in her other two jobs combined. Much more. It had been so freeing to quit her cleaning job. Walking in the office buildings at night when no one was there had been boring, freaky, and just plain disgusting at times.

Whoever said that professionals were neat freaks who always picked up after themselves obviously never had to clean their offices after they'd eaten two meals without bothering to throw anything away.

Although the food was gross, and finding it half in the garbage and half on the floor was bad, it wasn't nearly as bad as finding spent condoms. Just thinking about it had her shuddering.

Addison walked into the kitchen to take a breather. One of the three cooks looked up, his smile wide as he spotted her.

"What's up, Addy-girl?"

Marcus was so fun-loving and cheery that she didn't

mind his nickname for her. His skin was a deep black, his head shaved, and his face in a perpetual smile. As far as she could tell, nothing got Marcus down.

"What is it with tonight?" she asked as she put a hand on her lower back to stretch it. "It's like the crazies have come out."

Marcus laughed as the other two cooks joined in. Marcus plated a dish of blackened catfish and winked at her. "It's a full moon, girl. Didn't you know?"

"I didn't." She knew animals reacted weirdly during full moons. There were more dead animals littering the roads during a full moon than any other time of the month.

Marcus motioned her over, his smile dropping. Once she was near, he leaned in and said, "Let one of us walk you home, Addy-girl. It's not a night to be out by yourself."

She looked into his black eyes and saw that he wasn't teasing her. He was truly worried. And it made her nervous, especially after Minka's announcement that afternoon. "All right," she agreed.

With his smile in place once more, Marcus nodded. "Good, good."

She watched as he turned and effortlessly sliced a grilled chicken breast into pieces before putting them in a bowl of pasta and tossing them. Addison pivoted and walked back into the bar. That's when she saw Riley by herself looking ragged and dead on her feet. Addison quickly went to help.

"Thank you," Riley said with a grateful look.

For the next two hours, Addison went from one person to another filling drinks and getting the waitresses their drink orders. It was after one in the morning before she was able to take a breather and survey the place. Many of the patrons were gone, but there were still a few tables occupied.

"Think you can handle them?" Riley asked. "If so, I'll send two of the waitresses home."

"I've got them covered," Addison said as she walked from behind the bar to check on the tables.

She was clearing dishes from a table of two couples, when one of the women gasped and dropped her glass. Addison looked up to see the customer had gone pale, her gaze beyond Addison.

Addison spun to the door to see a woman dressed in all white standing just inside the bar. Her dark skin was in direct contrast to her attire and brought all the attention of the bar to her. The woman's gaze scanned the bar until she spotted Addison.

A shiver went through Addison when the woman smiled and then walked to a table. It was only belatedly that Addison realized the woman wasn't alone. A tall black man, dressed in white pants and white shirt, followed close behind, only sitting once the woman had chosen a chair.

It was one of those rare times when Addison would have gladly turned the table over to someone else, but she had told Riley she could handle things alone.

Her legs were wooden as she walked to the kitchen. She put the dirty plates in the sink and hurried back out to the front to clean up the broken glass, but Riley was already taking care of it. That left Addison with nothing else to do but go to her new table.

With her best smile, she stopped at the table. "Welcome to Gator Bait. What can I get for y'all this evening?"

The woman watched her with a half smile, the kind that gave the impression that she knew something

Addison didn't. Her black hair was done in dozens of tiny braids that fell to her waist. With her flawless dark skin and high cheekbones, the woman was spectacularly beautiful.

"Things have improved for you since coming to work here, Addison," the woman said in a rich voice that seemed to fill every inch of the bar.

Addison swallowed as she gripped her pencil tightly. "Do I know you?"

"Not as of yet, but I know you."

"How?"

The woman's smile grew a fraction. "Where are the LaRue brothers?"

"I don't know. It's not my business to keep up with them," Addison replied stiffly. Her arms began to shake from keeping them locked in place as she waited to take down the order. "Now. What I can get you to eat or drink?"

"I didn't come for the food," the woman said and crossed one leg over the other, her long skirt moving fluidly. "And I can get drinks anywhere."

Addison lowered her arms to her sides. She knew the woman was goading her into asking the question, and even though she knew it would be better to walk away, she asked, "Then why are you here?"

"For you."

Addison was so shocked she took a step back. Who was the woman, and why had she come for her? Addison knew enough to recognize the woman's attire as that of the Voodoo culture. It was a religion she knew nothing about, other than the fact that it could be dangerous in the wrong hands. She didn't want – or need – to know any more than that.

"Is there a problem?" Riley asked as she walked up

beside Addison.

The woman's smile grew slowly as she took in Riley. "I didn't expect to see a Chiasson here in New Orleans. I don't think my day can get any better."

"Who are you?" Addison asked.

The woman bowed her head as she slid her gaze from Riley to Addison. "I'm Delphine." She narrowed her eyes on Riley. "Didn't your brothers mention me?"

Addison glanced over at Riley to see her shaking with anger. Her lips were pinched tight and her hands were fisted at her sides.

Delphine threw back her head and laughed. "Ah. I see that they have. I wonder, do your brothers know you're here? I imagine they would do everything in their power to keep you out of New Orleans after my last encounter with them. . Hmm. Is there discord in the tight Chiasson clan?"

"Get out," Riley said between clenched teeth. "Now."

Delphine rose to her feet. Her smile was gone, but a look of utter delight shone in her black eyes. "You should know more about your employers, Addison. Just being associated with such...people...could get you in all sorts of trouble."

With that, Delphine turned on her heel and walked out of the bar.

Everyone breathed easier once Delphine was gone. Everyone but Addison, that is.

"Don't listen to her," Riley said as she stared at the closed door. "She has a grudge against my family that started with the LaRues, and has since expanded to encompass the Chiassons."

Addison swallowed and rubbed her hands over her arms. "Why did she seek me out?"

"To frighten you." Riley faced her and flashed a quick grin. "Delphine is a Voodoo priestess. Watch yourself around her."

They turned to find Marcus behind them, his face a thunderous expression of fury and hate. "Riley is right, Addy-girl. Delphine is bad business."

Addison didn't need either of them to tell her that. She sensed it the moment she saw Delphine, but that still didn't stop the priestess's words from running through her head over and over again.

CHAPTER SIX

Addison couldn't wait to call it a night. She was exhausted both physically and mentally. Delphine's visit had only agitated things, and she was more than curious where Myles and his brothers were. When she'd asked Riley about it, Riley had shrugged it off and said the boys needed a night off.

Addison walked out the back with a bag of trash. She opened the dumpster and threw it in. After she dusted off her hands, she looked up at the sky, but she couldn't see the moon from where she was.

She turned to go back inside when a man stepped out of the shadows. Addison took a look at the door, but the narrow alley prevented her from having enough room to go around him and reach the door. If anything happened, no one inside would hear her scream with the music blaring.

Addison glanced over her shoulder to the wooden fence that locked her in. She didn't think she could climb it fast enough or open the locked gate quick enough to get away.

She took in the man. He was on the short side and thin-framed, but there was something about him that made her wary, something that made her think he was much stronger than he looked.

"Here's the morsel I've been looking for," he said with a smile.

His skin looked pale in the light flooding the alley. His eyes were in shadow, but she knew they were trained on her as he began to move toward her. Addison backed up, her heart pounding in fear.

The man smoothed his hand over his slicked back, dark brown hair. "You're all that's being talked about." He licked his lips. "I'm famished."

"I can get you some food," she hurried to say.

Apparently he thought that was funny because he laughed. "Take a look at my clothes, sweetheart. Do I look as if I can't afford whatever it is I want?"

"You said you were hungry."

"Oh, I am." He peeled back his lips and his eyeteeth lengthened.

Addison had her second shock of the night, and it brought her up short, halting her retreat. Surely it was some trick of the light.

Minka had said there were vampires.

Oh, God. She was going to die from a vampire bite. The terror that consumed her locked her limbs so she couldn't move for a moment. Addison stumbled backwards against the fence, a scream welling in her throat.

Then a flash of dark fur sped from over her head. She yelped as something large and furry landed in front of her, a low, menacing growl emanating from it. The vampire took a step back and hissed. Addison wanted to think it was a dog, but there was no denying that she was looking at a wolf – a very large, very scary wolf.

Its body was low to the ground as it snapped its jaws at the vampire and issued another growl. For a second, Addison thought the vampire would leave, and then she realized the wolf had no intention of letting it go anywhere.

She plastered herself against the fence, praying the wolf didn't see her. Addison's hand shook as she tried to open the gate to her right. The jiggle of the metal caused the vampire's gaze to shift to her.

Her breath locked in her chest. Then the wolf turned its head to her and she saw into yellow eyes that seemed to glow from within. She was taken aback by the fierce beauty of the wolf. The next second, the wolf surprised both her and the vampire when it launched itself at the man and locked its powerful jaws around the vamp's neck. The yells from the vampire were drowned out by the growling of the wolf.

Addison screamed and focused on getting the gate open because she knew she was getting a first hand look at a werewolf. It took her a moment to realize it was suddenly as quiet as death around her except for the thump of the music from within the bar.

She closed her eyes, both of her hands still on the gate latch that refused to open. Addison slowly turned her head and looked over her shoulder.

The wolf was off to the side, standing over the dead body of the vampire that was turning gray and crumbling before her eyes. She lifted her gaze to the wolf and took a good look at its chocolate brown fur. It wasn't just more muscular than a normal wolf, but taller, as well.

It was no longer growling. It simply stared at her as if it were waiting on something.

"Thank you," she whispered.

From its position, it leapt over the fence with nary a sound. Addison gulped back a yelp of surprise and then hurried around the dust of the vampire as fast as she could before rushing into the kitchen.

All Addison wanted to do was get the night over with so she could try and sleep. Perhaps then she could forget all that she'd witnessed.

When she walked back into the front of the bar to finish cleaning off the tables, Riley stopped her by grabbing both of her hands. "You're shaking," Riley said. "What happened?"

Addison wasn't sure if she could tell Riley about what had happened. She didn't want anyone thinking she belonged in a loony bin.

"Addison, please," Riley urged.

"There was a man out back."

Riley frowned and glanced at the kitchen. She released Addison and strode to the back. Addison followed her outside. With one look, Riley walked to the last bit of ashes from the vampire. She knelt down and touched something on the ground.

Her gaze lifted and locked on Addison. "By the paleness of your face, I'm gathering you saw this?"

Addison nodded.

Riley sighed and got to her feet. "What happened?"

The acceptance on her face sent Addison's head spinning. She wrapped her arms around her middle. "You accept this as if you've known. You're not shocked there is a pile of ash there, and you know what it is."

"I could've lied to you, pretended I didn't see anything and waited until you left to get a better look. But I didn't. I do know about vampires, demons, witches-"

"Werewolves?" Addison asked.

Riley hesitated for a heartbeat. "Yes."

"That's what got the vampire."

Riley jerked her thumb over her shoulder to the fence. "I saw the fresh claw marks."

Addison dropped her head into her hands. "I can't believe I'm standing out here talking about werewolves and vampires. I've lived in New Orleans all my life. All of those rumors were just to keep the tourists coming."

"How I wish that were true." Riley came to stand beside her. "You're freaked out, but not nearly as much as I would've expected."

Addison dropped her hands and looked up. "This has been a really weird day. I was approached earlier by a fortune teller who said she saw a vision of me being chased by a werewolf."

"What?" Riley exploded. "Did she say werewolf?"

"She said wolf, but she said she was confused because she knew the wolves around the Quarter and said that they protected people." As Addison learned first hand that evening. "But she warned me that I was in danger."

Riley grunted and crossed her arms over her chest as her frown deepened. "That's obvious by Delphine's visit tonight. Someone is taking an interest in you, Addison, and it's cause for concern."

"Really?" she asked sarcastically.

Riley's face broke into a smile. "I think this calls for a drink. Only Marcus is left. Come inside and tell me in detail what happened out here."

~ ~ ~

Myles watched Addison and Riley walk back into the kitchen through a slat in the fence. By the way Riley glanced over her shoulder, she must have guessed he was still out there.

He was glad he'd listened to his instincts and remained behind. Not even killing the vamp cooled the fury that raced through him. The vampire should never have gotten that close to the bar, and he wouldn't have, had Myles not been led on a merry chase through the Quarter after another group of vamps.

It wasn't unusual for the Quarter to be a hotbed of activity on a full moon, but he realized now that he'd been led away on purpose. The vamp had been after Addison.

But why? And what did the vampire mean when he'd said that everyone was talking about Addison?

More disturbing was the mention of Delphine's name, despite Riley whispering it. In wolf form, he could hear everything – even the frantic beating of Addison's heart.

Knowing Riley would keep Addison safe inside, Myles made another round of the area. He and his brothers certainly had their hands full tonight, and the longer it took for him to return to Addison, the more frustrated he became.

It wasn't until the first rays of sun lightened the sky that he was able to follow Addison and Riley's scent, though Addison's was stronger for him. He loped along the streets, staying hidden until he came to Rue Parc Fontaine. He peered down the street and saw Riley sitting on the hood of a bright green Jeep.

She spotted him and slid off the car with a grin. "Am I glad to see you," she said when he trotted up. "You saved her, didn't you?"

Myles stopped beside her and looked up to the second floor where he could smell Addison.

"She's safe," Riley said as she patted his back.

That could only comfort him so much, especially knowing that she was still in danger. A witch from the Quarter had told her she'd had a vision of Addison being chased by a wolf. That disturbed him.

"I figured you'd come," Riley continued as she bent down and reached into a bag set on the ground, then straightened with something in her hand. "So I grabbed some clothes. You can't be seen like that, cuz."

Myles took the jeans in his mouth and moved off to a secluded spot. He dropped the jeans and let the transformation back into his human body begin. It was always easier to revert back into human form than to shift into a wolf. He gritted his teeth as bones, tendons, and muscles returned to their true form.

Myles was panting, sweat covering his body when he pushed up on his hands and looked around to make sure no one had seen him. Then he stood and pulled on the jeans before walking barefoot back to Riley.

She smiled brightly, holding out a red shirt and a pair of brown leather flip-flops. "We can't have you walking around barefoot. You don't know what you could step on. And the shirt is a necessity. If women caught sight of you, you'd never make it back to the bar."

He chuckled and put on the shirt. As he slid his feet in the shoes, he cut his eyes to Riley. "Let's get back to the bar."

"I suppose you have questions?"

Myles waited for her to get the bag before he started walking. "Yep. I won't be the only one."

"I knew you were out there," Riley grumbled.

"Was Delphine really there?"

Riley nodded. "I heard about her from Ava, but I wasn't expecting to feel the evil of Delphine so strongly. It was like she was the center of it all."

Myles put his arm around Riley and pulled her against him. "You shouldn't have had to face her alone the first time. Shit. Your brothers are going to have my head."

"She knew who I was without even knowing my name," Riley said and rested her head on his shoulders.

They walked the rest of the way to the bar in silence. Riley was tough. She had to be as a Chiasson, but she had been doing things herself for so long that she desperately wanted someone to take some of the load off her shoulders. She just didn't comprehend that yet.

Myles walked them through the back of the building. As soon as they entered the kitchen, she pulled away, pushed her shoulders back and lifted her chin. Whether she knew it or not, she acted as she if she were going into battle, and in some ways she was – the battle for herself.

He stopped when he entered the front of the bar and spotted Court, Solomon, and Kane sitting with Marcus. Marcus was the only other person at the bar who knew what they truly were, and only because it had been Solomon who saved his life ten years earlier when a demon tried to possess Marcus as a teenager.

Marcus ran a hand over his bald head and met Myles's gaze. "Delphine was here for Addison."

CHAPTER SEVEN

Hours later, Myles lay in his bed with his arm behind his head staring at the ceiling. He was supposed to be sleeping, but his mind kept going over everything Marcus and Riley had told him about Delphine's visit and the fortune teller who spoke to Addison.

What was it about Addison that was drawing the eye of every faction of supernatural in the city? As far as Myles knew, she was a normal, every day southern girl. Obviously, he was wrong.

He rose and took a quick shower, not bothering to shave. He threw on a fresh pair of jeans, a black shirt, and boots before he made his way out of his apartment.

That was something the LaRues did differently than the Chiassons. They didn't all live in the same house. Solomon still lived in the LaRue house on the outskirts of New Orleans on the bayou. It was a grand place that was too big for one man, but Myles, Court, and Kane opted to reside in New Orleans, each of them taking a section close to each other but still allowing them to keep an eye on things within the factions.

Myles's place was an old warehouse he'd bought six years before and converted into large studio apartments. He owned a car but rarely drove it since he lived close enough to Gator Bait to walk.

He pulled his keys out as he reached the bar. Just as he was about to slide them into the opening, he heard something within. Myles opened the door and stepped inside to find Solomon pulling chairs off the tables.

"Couldn't sleep?" Solomon asked.

Myles shook his head. "You either?"

Solomon grunted. "You know I don't sleep."

It was true, and something they rarely spoke about. "I can't figure out why Addison is so important to the factions."

"Did you ever stop to think it's because she came to work here?"

Myles walked behind the bar and poured himself a cup of strong, black coffee. "How many people have we had work for us through the years? Not a one of them have been singled out."

"True," Solomon conceded as he set the last chair in place getting ready for the midday rush. He walked to the bar and sat on a stool. "Something in her past, maybe?"

Myles shrugged. "Could be. I don't want to interrogate her about it."

"It's either that or we call in a favor at the NOPD."

Myles scratched his cheek and drank more of the coffee, hoping the caffeine would kick in soon. "I'll be surprised if she returns. After everything, she's probably too freaked out to come back."

"Making it harder for us to protect her." Solomon raised his brows and looked pointedly at Myles.

"Since when was I voted the one to watch over

her?"

"Since you can't take your eyes off her."

Myles couldn't deny that. He thought he'd been covert about it.

"We're wiser now," Solomon said as he rested his forearms on the bar and laced his fingers together. His dark blond hair was disheveled as if he'd been running his hands through it. "We made mistakes with M.... We made mistakes."

Myles looked away when Solomon couldn't even say the name of the woman he had loved. Six years hadn't dulled the pain of losing her – or the memory of the tragic way she'd died. "I hear there are two new females that arrived at the were camp in Slidell. Go take a look."

Solomon's gaze went hard. "We're talking about you, not me. The point is, Addison is going to need to be watched regardless if she comes back to work or not. A vampire was here to kill her. Delphine purposefully walked into our bar to talk to Addison on the night she knew we wouldn't be here. Last but not least, someone from the witch faction reading fortunes had a vision about her being chased by a wolf."

"I know all of it. You don't have to repeat it," Myles said testily.

"Apparently I do, to beat it into that thick skull of yours."

Myles finished off his coffee and set the mug down hard. "You think I don't know you're shoving me at her in the hopes that I'll give in?"

Solomon held his gaze for several long moments. "I think you're fighting every natural instinct to take her. I think you're going out of your way to ensure you won't give in to the desire. I think you want her more than anything else. Ever."

"I can't," Myles whispered.

"Because you're afraid of falling in love? Or afraid of losing her?"

Myles didn't think he was strong enough to endure what Solomon had. To have found love, then to have lost it in such a heinous way, was too much. Now, knowing so many factions were interested in Addison only brought the possibility home.

"Both," Myles admitted.

Solomon put his hands on the bar and stood. "It still doesn't change the fact that she's in danger. I'll have Kane watch her first. We three can divvy up the time. You don't have to be involved."

Myles clenched his hands into fists at the thought of his brothers watching Addison's every move as he stayed behind. It was for the best. At least that's what he told himself as Solomon started toward the kitchen.

"No," Myles said before Solomon could go through the doorway. "I'll talk to her. And stop smiling, you jackass. I can see you."

Solomon laughed as he disappeared into the kitchen. Myles sighed and decided to go over yesterday's numbers to take his mind off things.

Except he learned an hour later that nothing could pull his mind from Addison. He finally gave up and left the bar. With no destination in mind, he wandered the streets until he came to Jackson Square.

Myles ambled through the many artists displaying their wares. As he walked, he studied the witches set up as fortune tellers. There were more than ever before. Some were frauds, but some were the genuine article.

He spotted a young witch who was more interested in watching someone than pulling in clients who walked right past her. Myles followed her gaze until he saw none other than Addison.

Myles walked to the witch and sat. She jumped, her head swinging to him. Her eyes widened, indicating that she knew exactly who he was.

"Minka, right? You told Addison she was in danger," he said.

The witch had long, deep brown hair that curled. A bright pink piece of fabric was wrapped around her head with tiny beads in various shades of pink hanging across her forehead. Her eyes were pale brown ringed in black, giving her a dramatic, exotic look.

She leaned back, her black blouse hanging off one shoulder. One dark brow rose as she returned his stare. Then she crossed one leg over the other, her pink skirt hiking up enough to show black beaded sandals. "Because she is."

It took her long enough, but at least the witch was talking. "From a wolf?"

Minka looked away briefly. "As I told Addison, that's where it gets complicated."

"How?"

"I sense danger involving her, and I know that she's chased by a wolf, but I don't think it's the wolf she should be afraid of."

Myles glanced to where Addison shopped across the square. "What color is the wolf?"

"Brown."

"Then you've got it wrong, witch. I would never hurt her."

Minka's head tilted as she studied him. "No, you wouldn't. Does she know how badly you yearn for her?"

"That's none of your concern."

"So, that's a no," Minka said with a twist of her lips. "Why are men so stupid?"

Myles snapped his fingers at her. "Focus. I need to know who is after Addison. A vampire tried to get her last night, and Delphine paid her a visit."

The witch paled at the mention of the priestess. "Delphine? She went to Addison's apartment?"

"No. She came to the bar."

Minka whistled low. "After you and your brothers captured her and tortured her? Are you sure she's after Addison and not one of you?"

"We're not stupid. We know we'll always be in Delphine's crosshairs. I don't like her attention on Addison. How did she even learn of Addison?"

Minka sat forward and lowered her voice. "There have been whispers for a few weeks about someone who has enough power to put Delphine in her place."

"I know who she is, but she's not in New Orleans," Myles said.

Minka shook her head, her brow furrowed. "I know about Davena. I was leading up to the fact that it isn't just Davena that's being talked about."

When she didn't continue, Myles gave her a flat look. "You can't come that far, witch, and not finish."

"Fine," she stated angrily. "But understand I put my own life in danger by telling you this."

"Just spit it out."

Minka looked around and suddenly became nervous. "Not here," she whispered.

Myles sat back and held out his hand. "You're a fortune teller, right? What better way to cover up what we're talking about than by reading my palm?"

"You're nuts," she grumbled but cupped his hand in both of hers. She ran a finger along his palm, her gaze focused on his hand. "They're still watching."

"Who?"

"My people. They don't want to be involved."

Myles looked at a table a few feet away to find a woman watching them. As soon as their eyes met, she hastily looked away. "Why?" he asked Minka.

"They say it isn't our fight." Her fingernail lightly scrapped down his palm. "I haven't told them what I saw, but they know something is up."

He leaned his head down as if intently watching what she was doing to his palm. "Ignoring it won't make the situation go away."

"No kidding?" she replied, her words dripping with sarcasm. "I also can't make myself see anything."

"Tell me what you know," he urged softly.

She met his gaze and then sighed. "The word is that Delphine is worried. She needs to make a sacrifice of someone pure in spirit, as well as a witch, to boost her power."

"Addison isn't a witch," Myles said, his other hand gripping the side of the table. "She must be the one pure in spirit."

"That's the conclusion I came to yesterday. I don't know why I saw you chasing her though."

He shrugged. "One thing at a time. If the other factions know Delphine's plan, then that could be why the vampire tried to kill Addison last night."

"Addison isn't just a good soul. She's truly pure in spirit. Unlike most of us, she really is spiritually clean, blameless and unstained from guilt Even when she would have a right to, she harbors no thoughts of revenge. There aren't a whole lot of those around, especially in the city. No one wants Delphine to gain more power. She has too much as it is," Minka said looking up at him with a smile so she appeared to be delivering good news to anyone watching.

Myles smiled in return. "We couldn't kill her when we had her. You know that, don't you?"

"We know what she did to Kane, but if you thwart her in this, I have a feeling she'll come gunning for you."

"Better me than Addison."

Minka jerked, her eyes going milky as she stared at him unblinking. Her nails dug into his hand, causing blood to well from the half-moon shapes.

Myles surreptitiously looked around before he leaned forward. "Minka? Hey, witch? Talk to me."

Her lids closed and Minka took in a deep breath. When she opened her eyes, they were once more pale brown. She dropped his hand and began to shake. This time, it was Myles who took her hands in his.

"Talk to me, witch. What just happened?"

"I saw your death."

CHAPTER EIGHT

Myles released Minka's hands and sat back. "Death is part of being a hunter. It finds us sooner or later."

"This is sooner," Minka whispered fervently. "Why aren't you freaking out? I would be."

"You think anyone in my family has lived to a ripe old age? We've too many enemies."

Minka raised a brow. "Such a macho man. Why can't you say that you don't want to die?"

"Does anyone *want* to die, witch?"

All the heat went out of her words. "Some do."

Myles immediately thought of Solomon. Six years ago, Solomon had begged for death. He sighed and focused on the present. "What can you tell me about your vision?"

"You were injured badly when the vision started," Minka said.

"I need details, Minka. Where was I? Who was I fighting? What were the injuries?" he pressed.

She slid her hands into her hair near her temples and closed her eyes. "There were trees and grass around you. I couldn't see the wounds, just blood. So much blood."

Myles leaned forward and lowered his voice. "Could you see who I fought?"

"No," she said with a shake of her head. Her eyes flew open as she dropped her hands. "You were in wolf form."

"Good. That will help. Did you get a look at what killed me?"

"A silver blade."

Damn. That really would end him for good. Myles stood and fished out two twenties from his pocket. He tossed them on the table to make their exchange look legit. "Thank you. The LaRues owe you. If you ever need anything, you come find us, witch."

He walked away with the new information rolling around in his mind. If he was going to die soon, it put things into a new perspective. Since Delphine was involved, there was a chance that his life could end that very day.

Myles stopped at the edge of the sidewalk, his gaze searching for Addison. He found her looking through a stack of paintings. If he was going to die, he was going to die knowing the taste of Addison's kiss.

~ ~ ~

Addison tried to tell herself she'd returned to Jackson Square to fill the time, but the truth was that she hoped Minka had more information. Addison hadn't worked up the courage to go to Minka herself yet. But she was working on it.

She was flipping through some paintings when one caught her eye and she paused. It was a painting of the

Quarter at night, a large, full moon rising. It was a big piece, one that would look amazing over her bed.

Addison knew she shouldn't spend any of her money on something that wasn't a necessity, and yet she wanted the painting. She glanced at the price and cringed. It was much more than she wanted to pay, but every time she tried to put it down and walk away, she couldn't.

"Find something you like?" asked a deep voice behind her.

A shiver went through her as she recognized Myles's voice. She turned her head to him. "Just browsing."

His crooked smile told her he knew she was lying. "I know the painter. He's good. I like his view of the city."

"Yes." Addison made herself set the painting down.

"I hear the bar was packed last night. Riley should've called one of us in."

It might have been Addison's imagination, but she had the feeling Myles knew everything that had happened the night before. "We handled it."

"So I hear. I also heard there was a dangerous visitor to the bar."

Addison wasn't sure if he was talking about the vampire, the wolf, or Delphine. "Uh huh."

"So, Delphine didn't frighten you?" he asked with a narrowed gaze.

She shrugged and started walking. Myles fell into step beside her. "She was definitely freaky. The way she looked at me made me feel as if someone had walked over my grave."

"Delphine isn't someone you need to mess with. At all."

"I'd love to take your advice, and I wish I'd have known that before she came into the bar."

"Yeah," he said tightly. "She knew we weren't there and waited until then to pay you a visit."

Addison glanced sideways at him. "It's all right. Riley and Marcus got her to leave. I'd still love to know how she knew my name."

"What do you know of Voodoo?"

"I know it can do very bad things."

Myles caught her gaze as they walked. "There are many rumors spoken in our city, but the ones about Delphine are true. She cursed Kane not that long ago, and she's not fond of our cousins."

"I kinda got that by the way she spoke to Riley."

He smiled and stopped to put his hand on her lower back to move her out of the way as a group of tourists walked past. "Delphine has killed many people," Myles leaned down and whispered in her ear.

Addison's body heated at his touch, and her heart skipped a beat when his warm breath fanned her neck.

"It's not good if she's put her focus on you." He fingered a strand of her hair.

She looked up at him, caught in his mesmerizing blue gaze. "She isn't the only evil in the city."

"No, but she's one of the most dangerous. She's unpredictable and power-hungry."

Addison licked her lips. Her stomach flip-flopped when his gaze lowered to her mouth. She held her breath when he leaned forward slightly.

God, yes. Please kiss me.

As if realizing where they were, Myles looked around. "You need to be careful and vigilant. Delphine could be watching now."

Addison was still trying to bring her body under

control, and he expected her to think? And if he could do that to her with a near kiss, what would he do to her if they ever did share a kiss?

Myles's gaze looked over her head, his face becoming hard. He then took her hand and hastily led her away. "It looks like my words are coming true. You're being followed."

Addison looked behind her as Myles pushed his way through the crowd. She spotted two men in all white hurrying after them. She gripped Myles's hand and had to jog to keep up with his long strides. Not once did he stop or slow. Addison had no idea where they were going, and she didn't care as long as she got away from the two men.

To her surprise, Myles pulled her beneath the iron arch of one of the city's famous cemeteries. If she thought he would halt then, she was wrong.

They meandered through the tombs until he suddenly stopped and pushed her against a crypt. He put his fingers to his lips. Addison nodded, gulping in air as she wiped the sweat from her face.

Something felt odd at her feet. She looked down to see her sandal had broken. How it remained on her foot during their flight she had no idea. Her gaze lifted to discover Myles was gone. Addison rolled her eyes and sank down on the stones to try and see if she could repair the shoe enough to get her to a store before her shift.

The crunch of stone made her head jerk up, and she spotted one of the men who had been following her. Sweat ran down his black skin, a smile curving his lips when he saw her. He let out a whistle, and a moment later, the second man joined him.

Addison opened her mouth to scream. Before a

sound could escape, Myles came out of nowhere, moving with lethal speed as he punched the men with his fists and elbows. In a matter of seconds, both men lay unconscious at her feet.

Myles held out his hand, barely breathing hard. "I'm thirsty. How about you?"

She blinked up at him. "How did you do that?"

"Years of training and living in the Quarter."

Addison took his hand and let him pull her up. She hadn't taken two steps before her sandal fell off. With a curse, she picked it up and began to walk with one foot bare.

One minute she was standing, and the next she was in Myles's arms. She locked her arm around his neck, her broken shoe forgotten.

"What are you doing?" she asked.

He gave her a droll look. "What does it look like?"

"You can't carry me all the way to the bar?"

"Wanna bet?"

She had seen his muscles through his clothing, but there was nothing like feeling the hard sinew under her hands. There was no doubt he could carry her. It wasn't that she minded being there, quite the opposite in fact, but it was embarrassing. Or it should be.

Her body heated from more than just the August sun.

"See?" he asked with a wink. "It isn't so bad."

She licked her lips, pulling her mind away from his close proximity. "How did you know I was followed?"

His mood darkened as a frown formed. "I didn't. At least not until I began to realize how easily they could snatch you off the street."

"I've never felt unsafe before. I don't like this." When he didn't respond, she asked, "How do you know about Delphine?"

"Everyone knows of her."

"Including the vampires?"

His gaze jerked to hers, but there was no shock or surprise reflected at her words. "Everyone."

"I didn't."

Myles looked away. "You do now."

"What aren't you telling me? Why didn't you freak at my mention of vampires?"

A muscle in his jaw jumped. She was so close to his face that she wanted to touch his cheek and feel the scrape of his shadow beard beneath her fingers. Addison gave in to the urge to touch him and smoothed her fingers along the blond hair at his temples. The strands were warm from the sun, and soft.

"Riley knew of them, which means you do, too. You also know what happened to me last night. Were you looking for me today?"

He sighed loudly and stopped. "Yes, I was looking for you, but not only because of last night." He released her legs and slowly lowered her until her feet touched concrete. "I know of the vampires. I know a lot of things you're better off not knowing."

She stared into his bright blue eyes. Despite everything he'd said, she focused on the one thing that made her heart pound. "Why else were you looking for me?"

"For this," he said as he slid a hand around her neck and pulled her against him as his mouth descended upon hers.

Addison rose up on her tiptoes and wrapped her arms around him. The fire, the uncontrollable need in his kiss sent her spiraling into an abyss of desire so deep she knew she never wanted to climb out.

His moan, so full of yearning, made her knees weak. He then tilted her head to the side as his tongue slipped past her lips. The world melted away, vanished. She was unprepared for the intensity of the kiss, the force of the passion that flared between them.

He deepened the kiss and she tightened her arms. She had to be closer to him, to feel his skin. Once she found the hem of his shirt, she skimmed her hand beneath and connected to his rock hard abs.

Myles pulled back, ending the kiss to stare down at her with eyes blazing with desire. "I've wanted to do that for awhile."

"What took you so long?" she teased.

Except he didn't smile in return. In fact, he looked sad.

Myles threaded his fingers with hers and turned her around. Addison saw then that they were at the bar. Had she been so wrapped up in him that she hadn't realized where she was? He led her inside, and it took her a minute to adjust to the dim light of the bar after the bright sunlight.

"What the hell happened?" Riley said as she hurried around the bar.

"Delphine sent some men," Myles answered.

Addison shifted her gaze to a table where the other three LaRue brothers sat. Solomon looked at their joined hands before lifting his eyes to her. She waited to see what he would do, and when Solomon sent her a small smile, she was able to breathe again. Because, somehow, she knew her best chance to survive was with the brothers.

CHAPTER NINE

Myles didn't want to release Addison, even to Riley. He watched the pair disappear into the back where Riley had some shoes for Addison.

"So what happened?" Solomon bade.

Myles swiveled his head to his brothers. He walked to the small, round table and pulled out a chair, turning it backwards before he sat between Kane and Solomon. "I went to see the witch who told Addison she was in danger."

Court whistled. "You're a brave man. You wouldn't catch me dead talking to them."

Myles tried to smile at Court's jest, but he couldn't manage it. "It took some doing, but I learned why Delphine wants Addison."

"The fact the bitch wants her at all is enough to kill Delphine in my book," Kane said through clenched teeth.

Solomon glanced at Kane before he looked at Myles. "Well?"

"Delphine wants to increase her power. To do that,

she needs two things - a witch, and a mortal pure of spirit."

Court grunted and looped one arm on the back of his chair. "I don't have to guess which category Addison falls in."

"Exactly." Myles ran a hand down his face, deciding he would keep what the witch foretold about his death to himself. No need to worry his brothers.

Solomon studied him carefully. "What are you leaving out?"

"Nothing," Myles lied. "The witch said the other factions know of Delphine's plan and don't want her to get more power, so they decided to eliminate Addison."

Kane drummed his fingers on the table. "So others will be coming after Addison?"

"Possibly. If Delphine doesn't get to her first."

Court made a face. "She sent a clear message by going after Addison in the middle of the day. My guess is she heard about the vampire last night. Delphine isn't going to want to take another chance."

"It's not like Addison is the only one pure in spirit," Solomon said.

Myles shrugged. "According to the witch, she is in New Orleans."

"How many of Delphine's men were after Addison?" Kane asked.

"Three. Only two attacked. The other watched from a distance."

"You should've gone after him," Court said as he leaned one forearm on the table.

"And leave Addison alone for a fourth I might not have seen?" Myles pointed out.

Solomon held up a hand when Court started to argue. "Myles did the right thing. If Delphine wants

Addison bad enough that she's willing to snatch her in the middle of the day, then it could have been a trap."

"Y'all could've killed Delphine," Kane said as he stared at the table, both of his fists clenched tightly atop the surface. "Had I not messed around and gotten cursed, you could've killed her. You should have anyway."

Myles reached over and placed his hand on Kane's shoulder. "If we'd done that, you would've remained in wolf form forever."

"Only until one of our cousins killed me," Kane said as he looked at Myles. "Each of you would be free of Delphine now, and Addison wouldn't be in danger."

Solomon rested one of his fists atop Kane's. "Then we wouldn't have you. We made the right call."

"We sure as shit did," Court stated loudly.

Myles dropped his hand from Kane's shoulder when Addison and Riley returned. He couldn't stop staring at Addison's mouth. The kiss had been everything he knew it would be and so much more. He forgot everything, including where he was, when she was in his arms. Why did she have to be so damn alluring? Why did he crave her as if she were life itself?

He didn't care that there were no answers. He didn't need them. All he needed was Addison. What a fool he had been to push her away, to keep his distance. Now, he feared he wouldn't have even a day with her.

A blush stained her cheeks, causing him to smile because he knew she was thinking of their kiss, just as he was. He loved the way her hazel eyes looked at him, as if she wanted to devour him.

"I don't think it's a good idea for Addison to work today," Riley said.

Myles wanted to hug his cousin for her quick

thinking. His smile grew, even as Addison began to argue that she needed to work.

"Riley is right. We can't watch everyone Addison comes into contact with if she's working," Myles said. "She needs to be somewhere safe."

Like his place.

Addison glanced away. "I have to work. Not only do I need the money, but I took a shift."

"That I can easily take over," Riley said. She nudged Addison. "I'm sorry, but I think it's for the best. Delphine can't get her hands on you if she doesn't know where you are."

Solomon got to his feet. "Then it's settled. Myles, I gather you'll take Addison to your place?"

"It's warded," Myles said and stood, his cock already swelling with the idea of being alone with Addison.

Kane pulled out his cell phone. "As much as I appreciate the warding, I think it might be prudent to bring in reinforcements."

Myles looked from Kane to Court to Solomon and shrugged. "Your call," he told Solomon.

For long seconds, Solomon mulled over Kane's proposal. He inhaled deeply and gave a rueful shake of his head. "I'm going to regret this, but all right."

As Kane made the call to the Moonstone pack, Myles waited for Addison to walk to him. Once she was beside him, it was everything he could do not to pull her into his arms and kiss her again.

She had no idea how tempting her dark pink lips were, how irresistible her taste. Or perhaps she did. Maybe she knew the way she tantalized and seduced him with her soft touch and big eyes.

"Your place?" she asked, a hint of siren in her

voice.

Myles could feel the eyes of his brothers and Riley on him, and he didn't care if they could see the hunger, the yearning for Addison in his gaze. "My place," he whispered and held out his hand.

There was a smile on his face as she laced her fingers with his. They walked from Gator Bait together, no words spoken. None needed.

Myles was alert and wary as they strolled down the sidewalk. He was wound tight by the time they reached his building. After quickly punching the code to open the door, Myles ushered her inside and up the four flights of stairs, bypassing the elevator.

He unlocked the steel door and slid it open. "Make yourself at home," he said as he waved her inside.

"I love the space," she said looking around.

Myles shut the door and watched her. He looked around the large room with its fifteen-foot ceilings. He'd left the brick walls and the air vent piping exposed, using them as part of his décor.

His bed had burgundy bed curtains that he could pull closed to shut out the light from the many windows was against the far back wall. The kitchen was small but adequate. He had no cabinets, instead storing what little he needed on shelves.

There was a small table in the kitchen where he ate if he didn't take the food to his brown leather couch that separated the bedroom from the living room. Opposite the couch, a TV hung on the wall.

"It's amazing," Addison said with a smile as she looked over her shoulder at him.

"It's simple."

She stopped and turned to face him. "It suits you perfectly."

Myles locked and pushed off the door. "I've got movies. There's an Xbox if you prefer. I can also make you something to eat if you're hungry."

"I'm not hungry, I don't play video games, and I don't want to watch a movie." She pulled her purse strap over her head and dropped the bag on the couch.

Myles held his ground, afraid to move or utter a single sound and break the spell. Addison removed the too-big flip-flops while holding his gaze. He'd seen those amazing eyes up close. There were flecks of gold in her hazel eyes, and when she was scared, there was more green than brown.

"What do you want to do?" he asked.

She smiled a little shyly and glanced down. "This," she said and closed the distance between them before she kissed him.

Myles locked his arms around her and gave himself up to the fiery, fierce kiss. This time, he didn't have to worry about an attack. This time, he didn't have to end it.

He backed her across the space to the bed and lifted her up. A laugh escaped her as she broke the kiss and looked down at him. Myles carefully tossed her on the bed and quickly placed a knee on the mattress as he crawled over her.

"That look makes me feel as if I have butterflies," she whispered.

Myles paused. "What look?"

"This one," she said and placed her hands on his face tracing his nose, brows, jaw, and lips.

He turned his head to place a kiss on the inside of one of her arms. "Ah. You mean the one that says I crave you more than anything."

"Yes," she said breathlessly. "No one has ever

looked at me like that before."

"Stupid fools. Then again, they saved you for me."

He lowered his weight atop her as they kissed again. She began to tug at his shirt. Myles stopped kissing her long enough to yank it off. The way her body cradled his caused his blood to pound relentlessly with need. He wanted to take his time, to love her accordingly, but he'd spent too long fantasizing about making her his.

He rolled onto his back, bringing her with him. As he did, he pulled off her shirt and tossed it aside. Her skin was warm, soft. Her lips were enticing, tempting.

It took little more to remove her denim shorts, leaving her in nothing but her plain white cotton bra and panties. With a flick of his wrist, he unhooked her bra and slid the straps down her arms. It was Addison who pulled it from between their bodies and flung it. He returned her to her back and leaned over her.

"My God," he murmured as he looked down at her pert breasts and pink tipped nipples. He skimmed his hand along her flat belly and then up to cup one breast. "You're gorgeous."

Her blush stained her cheeks, her chest, and even her breasts. How one compliment could embarrass her only made him want more time with her. He watched her face as he flicked his thumb across her nipple. She inhaled sharply at first. As he circled the taut bud, her hips began to move.

She was a lovely sight, a mixture of innocence and seduction that was slowly driving him mad with lust. His hand moved to her other breast and teased the nipple until both were hard peaks. Only then did he bend down and fasten his lips around them, suckling first one, then the other. He used his tongue, and his teeth, to arouse.

Small cries of pleasure filled the area. With a nipple still in his mouth, he caressed down her stomach to her panties and then between her legs. His cock jumped when he felt the wet spot from her arousal.

It sent him over the edge. Myles turned his head away and closed his eyes as he struggled to get control.

"What is it?" Addison asked softly.

"I want you," he ground out.

"Then take me."

Her words, simply spoken, surprised him. He looked down at her and frowned. "I want to go slow, for you to savor every moment, but I want you too desperately. I can't do slow."

"Then don't."

CHAPTER TEN

Addison was on fire. Every place Myles touched made her ache, long for more.

His confession only made the flames of need grow higher.

With a moan – or was it a growl – Myles jumped off the bed and jerked off his pants. Addison rose up on her elbows and stared open-mouthed at the magnificent specimen before her.

Myles was sculpted to perfection. Every muscle defined, every inch of sinew rock-hard. She rose up on her knees and reached for him. His hands were clenched at his sides, his jaw locked as she ran her hands over his chest and shoulders. There were a few scars – more than he should have – on various places of his body. But she wasn't interested in the scars.

She was interested in him. In the skin so hot it scorched her, in the thick arousal that jutted between them. Addison looked at the muscles bulging in his arms and shoulders as she trailed her hand over his washboard stomach to his narrow waist. A quick glance showed his legs were as muscular as the rest of him.

Just as she began to close her hand around his cock, she found herself on her back once more. Excitement raced through her when he ripped her panties off and spread her legs. She trembled when he stared at her sex for long moments. Then he bent and licked her. She sighed, warmth spreading through her body. His fingers found her clit and rolled the nub between them.

Addison moaned and clutched the covers. The pleasure was too much, the need too great. She felt as if her skin were too tight, as if her body couldn't hold in the ecstasy that threatened to shatter her.

"Open your eyes," Myles demanded in a gravelly voice. "Look at me."

She forced her lids open and met his gaze. He stood holding one of her legs in each hand. His rod jumped, brushing against her sex as he knelt on the bed. He released one of her legs so he could take himself in hand and guide his cock to her entrance. She swallowed loudly, her legs trembling with the need to wrap around his waist.

Addison bit her lip as he pushed inside her, stretching her. He shifted his hips twice, sinking farther each time. The third time, he plunged inside her, filling her fully. She cried out, her back arching at the pleasure that rocketed through her. He fell over her, locking his arms around her. The next instant, she was gathered in his arms as he began to drive hard and fast. She wrapped her arms and legs around him, meeting him thrust for thrust.

He was relentless, ruthless as he pounded her body. She closed her eyes, desire tightening inside her and pushing her ever closer to the pinnacle of pleasure. She was reaching for it when it struck suddenly, sucking her breath with the force of the climax. Her body clamped around Myles's rod and convulsed repeatedly.

He rose up on his hands, his hips jerking faster. His bright blue eyes shifted to her. She was drowning in her climax and his eyes when they flashed yellow right before he threw back his head and shouted her name.

Her body was still pulsing with the orgasm when he pulled out of her. Seeing his cock wet with her pleasure and his seed made her realize they hadn't used any protection.

Myles fell to his back and reached for her. He tucked her against his body, their skin damp from the exertion. "I've not lost control like that in...well, ever."

"Ditto," she said with a smile. But it soon slipped. "Myles, we didn't use protection."

He was silent for a moment before his arm tightened around her. "I was so caught up in you, I didn't even think about it."

"Ditto," she said again.

"I'm sorry."

Addison turned her head to look at him. "It's just as much my fault. The blame doesn't rest on your shoulders alone."

He ran a hand down her hair. "You're one in a million, Addison Moore. I don't know what brought you into the bar, but I'm glad it did."

She looked down at his chest as she thought of that day that had changed her life. "At the time, I thought it was the worst day of my life."

"Worst?" he asked with a frown. "Why?"

"I had just received a letter telling me I could no longer get financial aid for the fall semester."

"Get a student loan."

"I have several, all extremely large amounts, but

they don't cover everything." She licked her lips and looked into his handsome face. "My mother died when I was four. I don't remember her at all except for pictures Dad kept for me."

"And your father?"

"A Navy pilot. He died in a training accident out in the Gulf when I was twelve. You know, I've never told anyone that," she said wondering what made Myles so different.

He touched her face gently. "I'm sorry. I know what it's like."

"You had your brothers. I didn't have anyone."

"There was no family to take you in?" he asked, surprise flickering in his blue eyes.

Addison shifted on her elbow, her arm bracing her head so she could play with his ash blond locks with the other hand. "I lived with my grandmother for two years before she died. My mother's brother took me in, but then he grew ill. They had three other children, and I knew I was a burden. I went to live with my dad's only surviving sister. I thought I was so lucky to remain near everyone."

"Did they mistreat you?"

"They never laid a hand on me. They were...cordial, but I never felt like I was a part of the family. They were very poor, but I didn't care. I had a house, food, and clothing. We scraped for every penny. I got a job as soon as I could just so I could have lunch money."

"My God."

She shrugged. "We weren't the only poor people, and compared to some, we were doing well."

"How long did you stay with them?"

"Until I graduated. Unbeknownst to them, I opened a bank account and was putting my money there. I had enough to cover an apartment, but not nearly enough for a semester of college. I took a little over a year saving every penny I could. Once I had enough money, I registered at Tulane and found a roommate."

Myles put his other arm under his head. "This sounds like the start of a happy ending."

"It should've been." It was supposed to have been. Addison swallowed and dropped her hand from his hair to rest on his chest. "I was able to get grants as well as student loans, but even all of that didn't cover everything. It took me working two jobs to get by, and that cut into how many classes I was able to take."

"Which extended when you should've gotten your degree," Myles guessed.

Addison flashed a grin. "Bingo! I applied for another grant over the summer for the fall semester. The day I came into Gator Bait for the first time I got a letter stating that I wouldn't be receiving the grant because my family made too much money."

"Wait, what?" he asked, his brow furrowed deeply. "You just said –"

"I know," she interrupted him. "That was my thought as well, but the letter went on to explain that the government learned my aunt and uncle were actually part of a money laundering ring years ago." She laughed lightly. "To think they could've paid for some of my college, that I didn't have to have two or three jobs to make ends meet, that I didn't have to sell my car infuriates me."

"It should."

She fell onto her back and looked at the ceiling. "I didn't expect a lot from them, but if they had that kind of money, I would have only asked for a little bit of it if

I thought they came by it honestly."

"What now?" Myles asked as he rolled up on his elbow to look at her.

"I'm working and saving money so that I can, hopefully, return to Tulane for the spring semester. I only have a year left."

"You never said. What are you getting a degree in?"

"Accounting." At his smile, a burst of laughter left her. "I forgot, you're an accountant."

He shrugged, grinning.

"Did you get your degree from Tulane?" she asked.

Myles leaned over and gave her a quick kiss. "We missed lunch, and I'm starving. How about you?"

"Yep," she answered as she watched him jump from the bed and pad naked into the kitchen area. She wondered why he hadn't wanted to answer her question about his degree.

She forgot about his non-answer as she looked her fill at his splendid body. If she thought he was going to cook, she was sadly mistaken. He got his phone and sent off a text.

"No cooking?" she asked when he turned back to her.

Myles laughed. "I burn everything I attempt to cook. I'm a disaster in the kitchen. It's so bad, Solomon has banned me from even thinking of cooking at the bar."

Addison laughed so hard her cheeks began to hurt.

"What?" he asked with a big grin. "You find that funny? Didn't you know there are those of us who can burn water?"

Unable to form words because of the laughter, she held up a hand, begging him to stop.

He was suddenly on top of her, his eyes twinkling

with joy. "You have an amazing laugh."

"I've not laughed like that in a long time," she said when she was able.

"You should do it more."

Addison was about to agree if it meant Myles was there, but the idea of hoping whatever was between them would be long-term was too soon. "You just like to see me laughing so hard I can't even talk."

"I like to see you laughing," he said suddenly turning serious. "I like to see you moaning. I like to see you climaxing."

Desire, only banked, flamed once again. With just words, he had her melting, aching for his touch. His head lowered, and she parted her lips for his kiss.

Just before their mouths met, something buzzed loudly throughout the room. Myles groaned in frustration and once more climbed off the bed.

He walked to an armoire that looked antique and opened the doors. He pulled on a pair of jeans. "Our food is here. I'm more than happy to see you naked, but if you want something to put on besides your clothes, feel free to dig in here. There are some old sweats."

Addison remained on the bed until the door slid closed behind him. Then she rose and made a beeline for the armoire. She found the old sweat pants but opted for a pair of cut off sweats that she had to roll several times at the waist so they would remain on.

Beneath the cut offs was an old sweatshirt that had the sleeves and neck removed. It wasn't until she pulled it on that she realized the bottom of the sweatshirt had been cut, as well. The steel door opened and she was only able to glance down at herself before she heard an appreciative whistle.

"Now I know why I saved those," Myles said.

Addison smiled and faced him. "These look older than you. I'm thinking I shouldn't be wearing them."

"I told you to help yourself." He set the bag of food on the table. "Those were my father's. When he died, I couldn't fit into them, so I cut them until I could."

She knew she shouldn't have put them on. Addison started to remove them when Myles's hand wrapped around her wrist. How had he gotten to her so quickly across the large expanse?

"It's all right," he said softly. "They look good on you. Besides, they were just collecting dust."

Addison lowered her gaze to his chest and noticed his scars again. She saw what looked like four slices cutting across his left side. The scars were old, and whoever had stitched it had done a good job. "What happened?"

"You know how crazy Mardi Gras can get. Come on. Let's eat," he said and tugged her after him.

Addison was beginning to think there was much more to Myles than he was telling her. Then she recalled how his eyes had flashed yellow.

The same yellow of the wolf that had saved her.

CHAPTER ELEVEN

Myles wasn't surprised when Addison fell asleep midway through the movie she had chosen after they'd finished eating the crawfish etouffee. He carefully lifted her in his arms and brought her to the bed. Myles laid her down and covered her with a sheet. Unable to turn away, he stared at her for several seconds.

Her short champagne blond hair fell against her cheek when she turned her head to the side. Myles gently moved the strands away. Somehow, he'd known making love to Addison would eclipse anyone from his past. And it had.

She was sweet, tender, brave, courageous, beautiful, giving, and trusting. He didn't want to lie to her, but he also wasn't ready to tell her who he was. What he was. It wasn't because he feared she wouldn't accept it. It was because he was terrified that she would then want nothing to do with him.

Myles ran a hand through his hair and turned on his heel to clean up what was left of their meal. He didn't take the bar receipts from the previous night out of the bag as he should, but instead, sat on the couch with his laptop.

Addison had told him some of her past, but he wanted to know more details. As difficult as it had been for her to share what she had, he was loath to ask more. So, instead, he went to the Internet.

It didn't take him long to find her father, Colonel James Moore, and the malfunction of his jet during a training exercise. There hadn't even been a body to recover. His search for Addison's mother took a bit longer since he didn't know her first name, but eventually he found where she died from ovarian cancer.

Addison's aunt and uncle took no time to learn about. The article he read explained how the couple had been under investigation by the FBI for years, but they'd been unable to get any proof until five years ago – when Addison had left.

Fury burned within him. The idiots lived in poverty because they didn't want to share any of their stolen money with Addison. She worked herself to death just to make a better life, when her family had the means to make it easier for her.

It was a good thing they were already in custody of the FBI because Myles seriously contemplated paying them a visit – in wolf form.

He wasn't rich, but he and his brothers were comfortable, thanks to the money left to them by their parents. The four of them had invested that money and recouped enough to buy the bar, leaving a little bit extra for each of them. Myles had invested his money once more and returned a much larger profit, which netted him the building. With his tenants, he was bringing in enough that he lived very comfortably.

Myles could give some money to Addison, but he knew she wouldn't take it. She had done everything herself so far, and she wouldn't stop now. He closed the laptop and set it aside. Then he rose and walked from window to window looking out to see if the wolves from the Moonstone pack had answered Kane's call.

A guy with dark hair reaching his jaw looked up from his post on the corner across the street and met Myles's gaze. Kane had the relationship and interaction with the pack outside of New Orleans, but Myles recognized another werewolf when he saw one.

He nodded to the guy who quickly moved into the shadows. Myles found three more wolves stationed around the building. Normally, the LaRues handled whatever cropped up in the city themselves, but they'd learned the hard way that when it came to Delphine, they couldn't do it alone.

Ever since Delphine had taken over as priestess thirty years earlier, the Quarter had gone to shit. The tentative peace Myles's parents had instituted between the factions after five long years was destroyed in a single night.

The peace hadn't been the only thing wrecked. His family had been, as well.

A sigh passed through his lips when he felt Addison's small hands wrap around him from behind. She rested her head on his back and held him tightly.

"You look as if the weight of the world rests on your shoulders."

He covered one of her hands with his. "It feels that way at times."

"Want to talk about it?"

It was never spoken about, and maybe that was the

problem. Maybe keeping it inside, letting it fester and rot only made things worse. "You never asked why we hate Delphine so much."

"There was mention of her cursing Kane." She shrugged. "I figured that was it."

Myles turned around in her arms and rested his hands on her small waist. "There are many reasons my brothers and I detest her. The fact she tortured one of our friends, Jack, for years, and then cursed Kane to try and kill Jack's daughter ranks pretty high. She also has an affinity for killing for the fun of it and keeping our city in constant terror."

"Why don't the police do anything?"

"She controls most of them."

Addison nodded slowly, a frown forming. "You want to kill her."

It wasn't a question. "More than anything."

"Why?" she whispered.

"Because she killed my parents."

~ ~ ~

Addison hadn't been prepared for such a statement. She stared up at Myles trying to find the right words.

"My parents worked tirelessly to bring about an accord between the vampires, demons, witches, wolves, djinn, and those involved in Voodoo. It worked. After three months of peace, my parents left us behind and went out to celebrate."

She didn't want to hear any more, and yet she couldn't tell him to stop.

"The restaurant was one known as neutral ground for all the factions. Delphine blew it up."

"Oh God," Addison mumbled, feeling sick to her

stomach.

"My parents were far enough from the blast that they weren't killed, just badly injured. My father had a shard of steel in his leg, but he still carried my mother through the rubble outside."

Addison closed her eyes, but the picture Myles painted was clearly visible.

"Delphine and her people were waiting for anyone who tried to get away. My parents were killed with a knife to the heart." He snorted, a rueful smile playing upon his lips. "I was watching TV with Solomon when we heard, and felt, the explosion. We woke Kane and Court up and went to see what had happened. That's when we found my parents. They were facing each other, their hands linked. They looked so peaceful that at first I didn't believe they were dead."

Addison covered her mouth as tears seeped between her lids and fell upon her cheek. The horror that Myles and his brothers endured was beyond imagining.

"You can conceive the chaos such an event would cause, and yet Delphine, clad in her white clothes, stood with her people watching with a smile upon her face. I tried to kill her then, but Solomon held me back. He'd seen what I hadn't."

She blinked open her eyes and sniffed. "What?"

"Delphine had sent men to kill us."

Addison shook her head, unable to fathom such a thing. "What? Why?"

"My parents weren't just powerful, they had a lot of influence in the city, and especially the Quarter."

The way he spoke, the conviction in his voice spoke volumes. If his parents were so active with the supernatural factions, then that must mean they were somehow a part of it. Suddenly, Addison knew to the depths of her soul that Myles was a werewolf.

She licked her lips and wiped at the tears. "Y'all obviously got away from Delphine."

"Not without some help," he said, his eyes looking over her head and going distant, as if he were lost in the memories. "Our parents had a lot of friends. Some human, some not. Together, they got the four of us out of the Quarter. An old witch who was close to my mother did a cloaking spell that kept Delphine from finding us."

"Where did you go?"

Myles looked down at her. "We moved around constantly, just in case. It wasn't until all four of us were strong enough to take care of ourselves that we came back to the Quarter."

"Were your parents' friends still around to help?"

His lips thinned slightly. "A few. Most were killed by Delphine."

Addison backed up, leading him to the couch. She gave him a little push so that he sat, a small smile playing about his lips. It did her heart good to see even a hint of his smile. It meant the memories hadn't kept their stranglehold over him.

His arms snaked out and wrapped around her. He pulled her back, toppling her into his lap. They looked at each other, sharing a grin. Myles tucked a strand of hair behind her ear before tracing the shell with the pad of his finger.

"You've not asked," he said.

"Asked what?"

"What my parents were. What I am."

His voice was low, as if he hated saying the words. "Are you embarrassed by what you are?"

"No," he said forcefully. "Never."

"Good. I've not asked because it's easy to deduce that you're some faction of the supernatural."

His bright blue eyes narrowed on her. "Which one?"

She trailed her thumb over his lip and recalled the flash of yellow. "Wolf."

Surprise flickered in his eyes before a frown marred his face. "How did you know?"

"When we made love...your eyes flickered yellow."

Myles's jaw went slack. "What?"

"Didn't you know they did that?"

"No. They've never done that before."

Addison raised her brows. "And you're always looking in a mirror when you orgasm?"

"No," he said gruffly. "But it's something a woman would remark upon, right?"

She had to agree with him. "Right. What do you think it means?"

"I'm not sure. I've never heard of it happening before."

With a sigh, she rested her head on his shoulder. "You know why Delphine wants me, don't you?"

"I do," he replied softly.

"Tell me."

His arms came around her. "Remember when I told you she went after Jack's daughter?"

"Yeah. That's when she cursed Kane."

"Exactly. That daughter, Ava, is engaged to Riley's brother, Lincoln. They live in Lyons Point near Lafayette, which has always been a hotbed of paranormal activity. It recently drew a witch who had been running from Delphine for years after watching Delphine kill her mother."

Addison clicked her tongue. "Delphine really needs to go and step on a Lego."

Myles burst out laughing, his chest shaking as it went on for a moment. He was finally able to take a deep breath. "Do you have even one mean bone in that body?"

"Yes."

"I doubt it," he said, still chuckling. "The witch, Davena, ended up being more powerful than Delphine expected."

"Delphine wanted to kill Davena, too?"

"That's what we all thought, but it turned out Delphine wanted to recruit her. Davena told her to kiss off in no uncertain terms, while demonstrating just how strong her magic was."

Addison lifted her head, trying to connect all the dots. "I gather Delphine wasn't happy."

"Until now, there hasn't been anyone to challenge her. Davena fell in love with another of Riley's brothers, Beau, so she has no interest in coming to New Orleans now. But she will."

"And Delphine is nervous," Addison surmised. "How does taking me help her? I don't have magic?"

He rubbed his hand up and down her arm. "You are pure of spirit."

"What? Not possible. Trust me on this, Myles. I've done bad things."

"Name one," he dared.

She opened her mouth, searching her memories. "Oh! I once left without paying for my coffee."

Myles looked at her as if that were ludicrous. "That's the best you can come up with?"

"I've said mean things."

"Like the Lego statement?" he questioned. "That's

not mean."

Addison pushed away from his chest and stood. "I'm not a good person. I've missed church, I've not left tips because I didn't have the money, I've said hateful things behind my aunt's and uncle's backs. Oh! And I even cheated on an exam. Well, only two questions of it, but it was still cheating."

"You're adorable," he said with a sexy grin.

She plunked down on the wooden chest that served as a coffee table. "Why does she need someone pure in spirit?"

"Between you and a witch, she can combine magic with purity and give her own power a boost," he explained, his face gone serious.

Addison lifted her chin. "Fine. How do we stop her?"

CHAPTER TWELVE

For hours, Myles walked the roof of his building. Addison had been like a dog with a bone. Once she learned the details, she wasn't content until she began to research. He gave up his computer and watched as she jotted page after page of notes from her findings. For his part, he was on the phone, calling friends to see if they could give him any more information than what the witch had already given him.

All he was able to discern was that Delphine was making waves with all the factions. No wonder the vampire came after Addison. The factions were worried, scared even. If Delphine gained more power, she would be unstoppable.

Myles braced his hands on the edge of the roof and leaned over the side. The Moonstone wolves were still on guard, though they were doing a good job of remaining hidden. They wouldn't be able to remain hidden for long, however, since night approached, and it was still in the phase of a full moon.

He couldn't believe Addison had guessed what he

was. After everything he'd divulged about his past, he assumed she would piece it together that he was part of a faction. But she had been so sure of her answer.

With a shake of his head, Myles chuckled. He knew his eyes had never flashed yellow before. Did she know it was him that killed the vampire? Was that why she wasn't afraid?

His mobile rang. Myles withdrew it from his pocket and saw it was Solomon. "Hey."

"Hey yourself. How are things?" Solomon asked.

"They're quiet. Too quiet."

"I know. I feel it too." Solomon released a breath. "The Moonstone pack will have to leave soon. I don't like the idea of you being there alone if Delphine shows up."

Myles continued to walk the perimeter of the roof. "This entire block is specifically warded against her. She can't get in here. As long as Addison stays inside, she's safe."

"And you?" Solomon asked. "What about you?"

"We're werewolves, brother. We protect the city and keep the factions in line. We have few allies and many enemies. It's a fact that no one in the LaRue or Chiasson line lives long."

Solomon was quiet for a moment, the sounds of the kitchen at Gator Bait coming through the phone. A moment later, the squeak of the back door sounded, and then silence. If Solomon had walked outside, then Myles wasn't going to like whatever he had to say.

"Spit it out," Myles said.

"I think Kane, Court, and myself should come help you."

Myles was flabbergasted. "And leave the Quarter unmonitored during a full moon? Have you lost your mind?"

"You've been looking at Addison for weeks, and today, that wistful look changed to one of possession. Wolves mate for life, Myles."

"No shit," he said icily.

"There's a very real chance that no matter what we do, Addison could die. Today, tomorrow, next week. She's not going to stay holed up in your place for long. Delphine will kill her. Trust me, Myles, you don't want to go through that."

Myles sat on the edge of the roof. "You want me to walk away from her?"

"I wan-"

Solomon's words were suddenly cut off. Myles stood, apprehension flooding him. "Solomon?" he yelled.

The sound of boards breaking came through the phone, and then the growl of a wolf.

"Shit!" Myles turned around in a circle, unsure of what to do. He didn't want to leave Addison, but if Solomon turned in the middle of the day, it was because he was ganged up on. And if Court and Kane were inside the bar, they would never know.

Myles slammed his hands down on the concrete of the roof edge, cracking it from his supernatural strength. He drew in a breath and opened his eyes to see the dark-headed wolf staring up at him.

He pointed to the entrance to the building, telling the wolf to watch it, and then he turned and jumped from roof to roof, making his way to the bar. Myles landed at the back of the bar breathing heavily. One look showed that a fight had taken place. All but one side of the fence had been obliterated. There were bits of white fur and blood about.

He leaned his head back and sniffed. Yet, he couldn't pick up Solomon's scent outside of the bar. Myles strode to the back door and threw it open. As he entered, he turned his head to the right and found Solomon leaning over the sink, bare-chested, washing blood off his arm.

~ ~ ~

Addison winced as she stretched her back. All of her research proved how dangerous a Voodoo priestess could be. Nothing she discovered gave her any hope that Delphine could be stopped with anything other than magic, however.

She rose from the table and walked around the space stretching her neck from side to side. Myles had gone to the roof to have a look around. He was trying to make her think it was all going to be all right, but there was no denying things were serious and everyone was on high alert.

Addison wished she had Minka's number. She'd give the fortune teller a call and see if there might be something she could do.

Her stomach rumbled loudly. A glance at the clock showed it was six in the evening. The sun wouldn't set for another two and a half hours, meaning there was plenty of light outside still. But it was dwindling quickly.

It was silly to think that evil only came out at night, but darkness seemed to hide evil so well. She hadn't been scared in the daylight, but with each tick of the clock's hand, she was becoming more and more frightened.

Her cell phone rang, startling her so that she let out a small scream. When she reached for it in her purse, her hand was shaking.

"Hello?" she answered.

"Addison?"

She closed her eyes with joy at recognizing Myles's voice. "How do things look from the roof?"

"Normal. I called the bar for some food about ten minutes ago. It should arrive any moment. I want to make one more round before I come in."

"No problem. I'll get the food."

She disconnected from the call and set the phone by the laptop. She didn't bother with Riley's flip-flops as she opened the door and hurried down the three flights of stairs. Addison tried to look out the glass window of the entrance door, but she couldn't see anything. She then opened it a crack and poked her head outside.

Movement from her side had her turning her head toward it when something froze her muscles in place. She tried to scream, but her airways were closed off.

~ ~ ~

"What are you doing here?" Solomon demanded angrily when he spotted Myles.

Myles gaped at him. "We have the threat of Delphine, then you're attacked while on the phone with me, and you want to know what I'm doing here? You're such a prick."

Solomon wiped his arms off with a towel before he tossed it aside. "I'm fine. It wasn't anything I couldn't handle."

"Who was it?"

"Two demons."

Court and Kane walked into the kitchen and

hurried to them. "What the hell?" Kane asked.

Solomon turned to the row of lockers behind him and opened one to pull out a shirt. "As I told Myles, it was just two demons."

"In the middle of the day?" Court asked incredulously.

Kane swung his head to Myles. "Did you leave Addison alone?"

"I don't plan on being here long," Myles said. "I'm returning now. And for the record, as I told Solomon, she'll be fine as long as she doesn't leave the building."

Solomon threw him a hard look. "You told Addison that, right?"

Myles started to say yes when he paused. Had he? He wasn't sure.

"Oh, fuck," Court mumbled.

Myles turned and ran out the back. He didn't bother going to the rooftops. He could get there just as fast on the sidewalks. His legs pumped hard as he went around throngs of people. He heard footfalls behind him and knew at least one of his brothers was with him. Myles didn't slow until he reached his building.

A glance across the street showed the werewolf was gone. "Damn," Myles muttered and quickly punched in the code to open the door.

He threw it open and raced up the stairs, Kane on his heels.

"Addison!" Myles shouted as he slid open the metal door.

Kane pushed passed him to the table. "Her phone is here."

"As is her purse, shoes, and clothes." Those were the only trace of Addison. "She's gone."

"The wolves might have seen something."

Myles wanted to hit something. "I left one watching the door, and he was gone."

"Griffin?"

"I don't know who the fuck he was!"

Kane came to stand in front of him and poked Myles in the chest. "You should. They're wolves, just like us."

"He's gone."

Kane made a sound at the back of his throat and walked out. Myles followed, shutting and locking the door behind him. Then both of them walked outside.

Myles stopped at the door when he caught a strand of champagne blond hair caught in the handle. Kane marched across the street. Myles looked up as he held the strand of Addison's hair in his fingers and saw Kane talking to two wolves. A moment later, Kane waved him over.

With a sigh, Myles walked to his brother and the Moonstone wolves. His mother had been a part of the pack, but after her death, the wolves scattered. Myles had never forgiven them for that. He hadn't been happy when they began to return to New Orleans five years ago.

"Tell him what you told me," Kane ordered them.

The youngest, a tow-headed teenager with eerie eyes so pale a blue they were almost white said, "We saw the woman taken by two men dressed in all white. Delphine was there, as well. Griffin followed them so he could come back and let you know where she was."

"Did they hurt her?" Myles asked.

Another of the wolves with brown hair and deep brown eyes nodded grimly. "Delphine did something to prevent her from moving, but your woman fought them."

His woman. Myles briefly closed his eyes as urgency pushed him. "I'm going to kill every last one of them."

"And I'll be there with you," Kane said.

The tow-headed wolf said, "We all will."

Myles frowned at the teenager. "Why? You don't know me or Addison."

It was the third wolf with a shaved head and tattoos peeking up from the neck of his shirt that shrugged. "Of course we do. Why do you think Griffin brought us back to New Orleans after our parents ran off? We shouldn't have left, and we're here to make up for the past."

"Just help me find Addison." Myles was in turns terrified and furious.

The emotions swirled through him with the force of a hurricane until he couldn't decipher one from the other. Like a fool, he'd kept away from Addison, and he refused to believe he was only meant to have one day with her.

Addison was his woman. Wolves did mate for life, and though she wasn't a wolf, his heart, his soul, his life was hers.

Myles nodded to the wolves. "Spread the word. Full moon or not, the Quarter is going to be invaded with us."

"Delphine still needs a witch," Kane said.

Solomon walked up with Court. "Which she already has."

"It's all over the Quarter," Court said miserably. "The witch was reading palms, went to get something to drink, and never returned."

Myles lifted his head when he heard a wolf's cry pierce the night.

"Griffin is calling," said the tow-headed wolf.

The wolf within Myles wanted free, to wreak havoc on those who would threaten what was his. "Then let's find him."

CHAPTER THIRTEEN

Myles rounded the corner of a building a half-mile from his place and spotted a shape move away from the shadows. The dark-headed wolf he'd seen earlier walked toward him.

Griffin looked to his men and gave a nod. "I wondered if you would accept our help."

"I told you we would," Kane said.

Griffin stared at Myles with his green eyes. "I followed Delphine. They've taken your woman to a cemetery."

"Which one?" Myles demanded.

"St. Louis number one."

Solomon snorted. "Of course. It's where the Voodoo Queen, Marie Laveau is buried."

"She's going to channel Marie," Kane murmured with a curse.

Myles didn't take his gaze from Griffin. "Delphine and her people likely heard your call. They'll be on the lookout for any wolf."

"Not if some of my men lead them away." Griffin

pointed to a black-haired werewolf. "Jaxon and a small group will cause a distraction for us."

"And me," replied the tow-headed teenager. Myles figured he was only about sixteen since he hadn't filled out yet as weres did in their late teens.

"Colt," Griffin said with a warning look. "I need you to return to the pack and get as many wolves as will come." Griffin's gaze swung to Myles. "I'm guessing the LaRues want to make an impact."

Solomon moved forward so that he stood beside Myles. "Without a doubt."

"This is going to cause a shit storm for sure," Court said.

Kane shrugged. "Everyone can kiss my sweet ass for all I care."

Myles turned his head to look at Kane. He'd missed his carefree and slightly reckless brother that had been more concerned with women and drink than their family legacy. What Delphine had done to him with her curse had changed Kane. He was still reckless, but there was a carelessness about him now, one that said it didn't matter to him if he lived or died. One that screamed for retribution and vengeance.

Myles was glad he wasn't on the receiving end of Kane's fury because Kane was a man with a mission, and nothing and no one would be able to stop him.

Why hadn't they realized it before? They should've recognized the lethal gleam in his eyes. Perhaps Kane had just gotten good at hiding it.

"The distraction needs to be big enough to cause Delphine to worry," Myles warned.

Griffin smiled menacingly. "I think setting her temple on fire might do it."

"Uh, yeah, that'd do it," Court said with a grin.

Myles wished now that he had gone out to the Moonstone camp and seen the weres. "How many do you think you can get?"

"All of them," Colt stated with conviction.

Griffin nodded in agreement. "They've been waiting for just such an event."

"What are you thinking?" Solomon asked Myles.

Myles looked at his brothers and grinned. "I'm thinking one of Dad's strategies. Surround and conquer."

"Simple, but efficient." Solomon gave a nod of approval. "It's worked before."

Myles looked back at Griffin. "Timing is everything. Delphine expects me and my brothers. I want your pack to hold back and wait for our signal."

"What will the signal be?" Griffin asked.

Kane slapped him on the back. "Trust me, you'll know."

With a look, Griffin sent Colt and Jaxon off on their missions. The third wolf remained, rubbing his bald head and moving to stand just behind Griffin.

"Give my wolves some time to get into place," Griffin said.

Myles looked at the sky and the growing darkness. "That might not be an option."

"Delphine won't start the spell until midnight."

Court crossed his arms over his chest. "And just how do you know that?"

"I know a lot about Delphine." Griffin looked over his shoulder at the other were. "We know a lot." He turned back to the LaRues. "This is my brother, Gage. Delphine didn't just turn our parents into mindless wolves that we had to kill. She has our sister."

Myles drew in a deep breath. "No wonder you were

so eager to help us with Delphine."

"Our parents made a mistake in running away the night Delphine went on her killing spree. Worse, they shouldn't have left the four of you behind."

Solomon was stony-faced as he said, "We turned out all right."

Myles couldn't stand around talking anymore. He had to see Addison for himself, to know she hadn't been harmed yet. "I'm going to the cemetery."

"Not now," Kane said with a hand upon his arm.

Myles looked from his hand to Kane's blue eyes. "Try and stop me."

"He's right," Griffin stated. "If you arrive now, it could ruin your plan."

Solomon turned on his heel. "I think there's another faction we need to talk to before we confront Delphine."

Myles hesitated while Court, Griffin, and Gage followed Solomon. After a moment, Kane released him and also followed. Myles blew out a frustrated breath and fell into step with the rest.

~ ~ ~

Addison woke to the pounding of her head. She tried to grab her temples, but her arms were jerked to a stop at her sides. A look down confirmed that she was tied with thick, course rope that already cut into her skin, rubbing it raw.

She laid her head back and looked up at the clear sky after glancing from one direction to the other at the huge stone monuments. The cemetery. Great. She wondered what she was laying on, then thought it was better if she didn't know.

Addison tried to yank harder against the ropes, but it only made her wrists bleed.

"Don't bother. You won't get anywhere," said a recognizable voice.

She looked around but didn't see Minka. "Where are you?"

"Behind you. For now."

That sounded ominous. "How are you here?"

"Funny thing, that," she said sarcastically. "I heard rumors about Delphine's plan, and even shared those with Myles. I didn't know I was the one she would take as her witch."

Fear snaked through Addison, turning her blood to ice. "Surely you can get us out of here, right? You have magic."

"I have visions."

"Obviously, you have more than that," Addison argued. "Why else would you be taken?"

"How very astute of you, Addison," Delphine said, her voice seeming to come from all around.

Addison turned her head to the left and saw Delphine's white dress seconds before her face came into view.

Delphine smiled and came to stand beside her. "It won't be long now, girls. Soon you'll be free of this world. You'll be doing something for the good of the Quarter."

Minka snorted loudly. "Just shut up with your crap. You're a murderer any way you look at it."

"That's right, Minka," Delphine said sharply. "Because every leader must sacrifice individuals for the good of the cause."

"Do people actually believe that drivel?"

Addison tried to turn her head when Delphine

walked behind her, but she could only catch a glimpse of white.

"I can make your death easy, or I can make it difficult," Delphine said in a hard voice to Minka. "You choose, witch."

"I'm not a witch!" Minka shouted. "I'd have to be able to do magic to be a witch."

Delphine chuckled, the sound getting louder as it went on. "Oh, how your family has lied to you. Do you think you were chosen on a whim? You have untapped potential they've been keeping from you."

"Don't believe her," Addison said to Minka.

Delphine's laugh was as hollow as her soul. "She'd better listen to me. There are many witches to choose from, but it was you I wanted. Imagine my surprise as I plotted to kidnap you, and one of your elders came to me instead."

If Addison was shocked, she could only imagine what Minka was feeling.

"It seems," Delphine continued, "that she was afraid of you taking over. She offered you in exchange for me leaving your coven alone for the next twenty years."

There was a squeak of rope before Minka said, "Liar."

But there was no heat in her words, as if she knew what Delphine said was true. Addison knew that feeling of betrayal, of having family turn their backs.

"And you, Addison." Delphine tsked and returned to stand beside her. "I didn't think a phone call pretending to be Myles would work with you. How easily you were captured. Did Myles tell you his entire building was warded against me?"

Addison felt sick to her stomach. She should've

known not to go outside. Myles would never have sent her down for food. What an idiot she was. And now, she was smack in the middle of something she didn't want to be a part of.

"To think of the lengths he went to in order to keep me from you." Delphine shook her head, her long black hair falling around her. "Tonight's ceremony is going to be one remembered for ages."

Addison glared up at the priestess. "Myles will come for me. He'll find me."

"Are you sure? A werewolf can't be trusted. I know because it was one of my ancestors who cursed the LaRues into being werewolves hundreds of years ago."

"He'll come." At least Addison hoped he would. They had shared their bodies only once. That didn't constitute a commitment, and yet she felt sure Myles would at least look for her.

Delphine turned and walked away, her laughter fading with her.

"Don't listen to a word that bitch says," Minka said.

Addison pulled on the ropes again. "Like you didn't listen to her."

"Because I know what she said is the truth."

Addison stilled, her eyes widening. "You know who betrayed you?"

"There are five elders of our coven. That narrows things down significantly. I didn't want to be a witch," Minka said softly. "I was unable to do even the simplest of spells, but I had visions."

Addison was quiet for a minute. "You spoke to Myles?"

"I knew he wouldn't tell you," Minka said with a loud sigh. "Men can be so...stupid sometimes."

She took exception to that. Myles wasn't stupid.

"He told me about Delphine's plan. He just didn't tell me how he heard of it. When did he talk to you?"

"This morning. Just in case you don't know it, that man has it bad for you."

That brought a smile to Addison's face. "The feeling is mutual."

"Yeah, I figured. Do you know who he really is?"

"He's a werewolf."

"Well, aren't you the smart one of the bunch."

Addison heard the smile in Minka's voice. "He'll come for me."

"Everything you've heard about wolves is true, Addison. Nothing will stop him from getting to you. Nothing."

"Delphine will kill him."

"Remember what I told you about the hunters? The ones who guard the city? The LaRues are those hunters. If there is anyone who can find a way, it's them."

Addison tried to swallow, but her mouth was bone dry. "I hope you're right."

"I am," Minka whispered. "I have to be."

CHAPTER FOURTEEN

It took two excruciating hours to talk three of the five witch covens and the Blood Mark pack into joining them. The witches hadn't been thrilled with the idea of joining two wolf packs, but the thought of Delphine gaining more power eventually swayed them.

"Stop pacing," Court said. "You're giving me a headache."

Myles threw him a dark look.

Kane gave a dismissive shake of his head. "It's the growling that's getting on my nerves."

"Leave it," Solomon said to Court and Kane.

Myles leaned against the building as he stared at the entrance to the cemetery. Was this how Solomon had felt when his woman was taken from him? His heart clutched because Myles knew he wouldn't survive if Addison were killed. How did Solomon bear the crushing weight?

"Just a little longer," Griffin said from beside Myles.

Myles looked at the leader of the Moonstone wolves. "Do you have a mate?"

"No," Griffin said with a laugh. "My father told us kids that we'd know when we found ours. I'm still searching."

"I didn't want one. Hell, I don't even know if she wants to be mine." Myles ran both hands down his face.

Solomon glanced at him from his position at the corner of the building. "She wants you. Trust me on that."

"Yep," Court said, nodding.

Kane stretched his neck from side to side. "We've seen it with our own eyes. She's yours, Myles."

"It's time," Griffin said and pushed away from the wall.

Myles felt his own wolf push against him. He began to remove his clothes, his breaths coming quicker and quicker. Griffin threw back his head as bones began to break and reform into that of a wolf.

The pain of the shift was indescribable. It battered them from all sides, taking their breath and ripping them apart from the inside out. Myles's wolf rose up quickly. Urgency pushing him, driving him.

He fell to his hands and knees. For the first time, he didn't feel any pain. His thoughts were centered on Addison. And killing Delphine.

When he opened his eyes, he watched his brothers finish their transitions. He saw the solid white fur of Solomon. Next to him was a wolf of inky black – Kane. On the other side of Solomon was Court with his tawny fur.

Another wolf trotted up. Myles eyed the mottled gray fur of Griffin. Griffin stared at Myles for a moment as Gage joined him before swinging his gaze toward the cemetery.

Out of the corner of his eye, Myles saw Solomon's ears flick. Myles lifted his head and listened. Only one other time in the history of the city had wolves descended upon it en masse as they were now. Tonight, the wolves weren't there to claim dominance but to free two innocents and stop a priestess.

It felt like an eternity before Myles smelled the first flames. Soon, sirens from the fire department and the police rang out through the city.

Myles and his brothers hid behind the building, the shadows deep enough to conceal them thoroughly. He peered around the corner and spotted one of Delphine's men dressed in all white come to the entrance of the cemetery to see what was going on.

Beside Myles, Kane growled, the sound rumbling through his chest. Solomon nudged Kane with his head to silence him.

The man ran back inside the cemetery, and just seconds later he and three others ran out and got into a car to drive off. That lessened who they had to fight by four, but Myles wasn't concerned with Delphine's followers. He was apprehensive about her.

One wrong move would seal all their fates.

He hadn't forgotten Minka's prediction of his death. If it happened that night, Myles wanted it to be after Addison was freed. He had to be smart, cunning, and ruthless. Those were the only traits that would save his woman.

Myles looked at his brothers. They lined up side by side and walked out of the shadows, through the parking lot, and across the street. They each had their destinations. Once they passed through the tall iron gate, they split up, slinking quiet as death around the tombs. Delphine's evil stench was suffocating, but it made her easy to track.

Myles went all the way to the back of the cemetery and then made his way toward Delphine, hoping he'd be the one to find Addison. His steps slowed when he heard Delphine's voice chanting. He shifted to his right and moved stealthily toward the sound. Myles leapt atop a tomb and crawled on his belly to the edge.

Delphine was without the white turban. Her hair was loose and hanging around her deep mocha skin. Where she was normally covered almost head to foot in white, this night she wore a white tank top that was thin enough to see her nipples through. Her skirt was long but sheer.

Myles had to force himself to remain still when he heard Addison's voice. A second later, she came into view with a man on either side of her, holding her. Minka was also held by two men as she was brought after Addison.

Delphine slowly raised her hands above her head. Flames surged, encircling the seven of them. Minka kicked one of the men, who then backhanded her so hard she fell to the side, narrowly missing the flames.

"Minka!" Addison yelled.

The men hauled Minka back up with blood running from her lip. Delphine began to sway, her eyes closed and the words coming faster. One by one, her followers appeared seemingly out of nowhere to form a large circle. They clapped slowly and hummed. Delphine's eyes suddenly opened, shining with an unholy red light. She pointed first one hand at Addison and then the other at Minka.

Myles growled in fury when Addison's entire body jerked and her lids fell closed. Minka mimicked her a second later. The men stepped back and out of the flaming circle since Delphine controlled both girls now.

Delphine's voice grew louder, her words incomprehensible. Myles could only watch as both Addison and Minka fell straight back. But they never hit the ground. They were stiff when their legs lifted, tilting their bodies horizontally.

"Our temple is on fire!" shouted a male voice.

Delphine stopped chanting and slowly looked around. "Go. Our home must be saved."

There was a commotion as half of the men and a few women rushed out of the cemetery to help put out the fire. By the way Delphine studied every shadow, she suspected the fire had been a diversion.

Myles hoped to catch her unawares, but that was no longer an option. She would be on guard now, prepared for whatever came at her.

She focused on Addison and Minka again and walked to stand between them. Delphine touched Minka's forehead and skimmed her hand down her body to her toes. Then Delphine repeated the movement with Addison, unintelligible words spilling from her lips all the while.

He snarled, his lips lifting. The hate was unbearable. It consumed him, devoured him. It had kept him going for years, but if he let it take him completely now, there would be no room for any other emotion like...love.

Delphine held her hands out in front of her, palm up. Out of nowhere, a curved blade made of bone appeared in her palms. Holding it in one hand, her other traced it as if it were an object to be worshiped.

When she held the bone blade high, her remaining flock sent up a cheer and continued clapping in a rhythm. Delphine turned to Addison first and gripped the bone in both hands above her head, preparing to plunge it into Addison's chest.

Myles leapt from atop the tomb between the worshippers and the fire, growling fiercely. Kane, Solomon, and Court each walked from their hiding places, their growls mixing with his. Delphine's people quickly moved to make paths for his brothers until they also stood at the fire facing the priestess.

"I knew you would come," Delphine said as she looked at each of them. "Which one of you is Myles?"

It was Court who snapped his jaws at her in response.

Delphine laughed. "Oh, this is just too simple. How silly of you LaRue boys to think the four of you could stop me. I'll kill these girls, and then I'll make sure to end the LaRue line once and for all."

Myles looked at Solomon from across the fire and nodded. Myles, Court, and Kane turned and charged Delphine's followers. Their screams filled the air. Though they never sank their teeth into a single one of them, their screams said otherwise.

With their signal to the Moonstone pack literally shouting from the rooftops, Myles turned back to Delphine, who stood glaring at Solomon. Just as Myles expected, the bitch was taking the bait. Because in her mind, only he would be the one to stand guard watching over Addison.

And Myles was, just not in the way she expected.

The screams of her followers intensified as Griffin's pack filled the cemetery with the witches right behind them. Myles threw his head back and let loose a howl.

Delphine turned in a circle staring in confusion and anger at the witches and wolves closing in on her people, standing atop tombs and filling the spaces.

"Enough!" Delphine shouted.

One young witch with dark red hair standing atop the tomb Myles had been on spread her fingers as she held her arms out at her sides. "You don't rule us. You'll never rule us."

The other witches spread their arms wide until they made one huge circle. Their eyes were locked on Delphine while they focused their magic. Delphine had no choice but to fight them.

It was time for the wolves. Myles was the first to launch himself over the flames and tackle Delphine to the ground. Right before he turned to go to Addison, he felt something sharp sink into his shoulder. Myles turned and snapped, but Solomon, Court, and Kane were already atop Delphine. Griffin and Gage soon joined in the fray.

Myles limped to Addison. He watched in surprise as both the girls dropped to the ground. Delphine had to conserve her power for herself, which freed Addison and Minka. He saw the blood on Addison's wrists and licked them to help spur the healing. When he lifted his head, her hazel eyes were open and looking at him.

"You came." She smiled and ran her hand over his head, sinking her hands into his fur. "I knew you'd come."

Myles nuzzled her until she had both hands around his neck. Then he stepped back and helped her into a sitting position.

"Nice trick there, wolf," Minka said with a groan. "Who the hell is going to help me?"

Addison reached over and helped Minka. Myles took the hem of Addison's cut off sweats in his mouth and tugged, trying to tell her they needed to go.

"I think that means we've got to go," Minka said.

Addison glanced at the wolves attacking Delphine.

"Yeah. The sooner, the better."

Solomon bumped against Minka and loped away. Minka quickly followed him. Myles ignored the pain of his wound and waited for Addison. As he ran behind her, he ensured there wouldn't be any other surprises from Delphine that night with the Moonstone clan and the witches attacking her.

While Solomon ran them down quiet streets until they were out of the city and into the bayou, Myles saw Griffin and his wolves with them. The girls would never make it to the Moonstone camp, and Myles didn't want Addison there anyway. He let out a sound that brought Solomon to a halt.

Minka and Addison stumbled to a stop, their hands on their knees as they bent over sucking in air. Myles circled them trying to think of a place to take them, because he wasn't sure how much longer he could keep going. His wound was weakening him significantly. Something that would only happen if silver were used.

Myles looked at Addison. At least she was out of Delphine's grasp now. There was no sense in telling his brothers about his wound. Nothing could help him now. He was dying, slowly but surely.

Griffin and his wolves spread out, checking the bayou while Solomon remained on point, too concerned about an attack to realize anything was wrong.

After a moment, Minka lifted her head and looked at Addison. "I know a place we can go."

"Where?" Addison asked breathlessly.

Minka straightened, a sad look coming over her. "The old Gilbeaux plantation. Or what's left of it."

Solomon let out a low growl and shook his head. Myles had to agree. That place wasn't fit for animals, much less the girls.

"It's where I'm going," Minka stated determinedly. "There's no other place for me. I can't go back to the Quarter."

Addison looked up then and shoved her short champagne locks out of her face. "No. There's no going back to those who betrayed you. What about one of the other covens?"

Minka was shaking her head before Addison finished. "Not possible."

"All right then." Addison slid her gaze to him. "We need to go to the Gilbeaux plantation."

Myles sighed and turned west, their course set.

CHAPTER FIFTEEN

Now that they had escaped the Quarter, Addison's feet were throbbing. She was afraid to look down and see the damage done. They had been walking for another hour, and she was weary to her bones.

Myles suddenly bumped against her, halting her. Was it her imagination, or was he limping? Addison looked up from the ground and heard the roar of an engine. Suddenly, wolves closed in tightly around her and Minka. She tried to hold onto Myles, but he slipped away, going to stand in front of the pack with a white wolf and a gray one.

A 4x4 truck drove through the pasture they were crossing and came to a sliding stop. The headlights blinded her, but Addison was able to shield her eyes enough to see the door of the truck open.

"Which of my asshole cousins thought it would be a good idea to leave me out of things?"

"Riley?" Addison said with a smile. "Is that you?"

"Addison? Are you all right?" Riley asked and jumped from the truck. She raced to her, the wolves instantly moving out of the way. Riley wrapped her arms around her and held tight.

"Yes, thanks to Myles and all the other wolves."

Riley stepped away. Her smile dropped as she glared at Myles and the white wolf. "That was shit. If I hadn't seen the group of witches walking down the street talking about all the wolves, I'd never have known. Then I found these two jerks," she said with a thumb over her shoulder.

Just then, a black wolf and one with tawny fur loped up.

"But that's family business," Riley said taking notice of all the other wolves. "Y'all must be from the Moonstone pack Kane talks about. Thanks for helping." Riley then shifted her eyes back to Addison. "Where are y'all headed?"

"The old Gilbeaux plantation," Minka said.

"Y'all look like death warmed over. Get in the truck. I'll drive while you give directions. There's some bottled water inside."

Minka didn't have to be told twice. She hurried to the 4x4 and climbed in the passenger side back door. Addison took a step and winced at something sticking in her foot.

"You don't have shoes?" Riley asked in consternation.

Addison shrugged. "I was taken without them."

Riley linked Addison's arm around her shoulder and helped her limp to the truck. Addison got in and saw Myles standing by her door.

"Want to ride?" He took a step back, causing her to laugh. "I'm fine. Let's just get to the plantation."

Once Myles trotted off and all the wolves disappeared into the trees, Addison closed her door and let out a sigh. She shut her eyes while Minka directed Riley through backwoods roads to the plantation. Addison didn't need to look. She knew Myles was near.

The certainty of that, of knowing that he would be there for her was as calming as it was wonderful. She'd never been able to say that about anyone before, and she was hesitant to even think it with him.

It wasn't because he was a werewolf and changed with the moon. It was because of who he was, what he did. He fought for the innocents of the Quarter, which meant he put his life in danger every day.

Her father had done the same, and look how he'd ended up. As much as that bothered her, Addison knew she couldn't walk away from Myles.

He was everything she hadn't even known she wanted or needed. His gentleness with her, coupled with his unwavering loyalty and defense of her against someone as evil as Delphine was staggering.

She didn't know where their relationship might lead, but she certainly wanted to find out.

"How does it feel to be the woman of a wolf?" Riley asked.

Addison opened her eyes and smiled. Minka shoved a bottle of water at her that she opened and drank deeply from. "It feels...right. Is that how it's supposed to feel?"

"I don't know," Riley said. "I think that could be the right answer for any couple."

"I just don't want to read too much into things. I suppose Myles was just doing his duty as a hunter."

Minka gave a snort of laughter. "Girl, I'm seriously about to knock you in the head. Didn't we have this conversation in the cemetery?"

"Yeah," Addison said. "It's just, everyone I've ever

wanted in my life has left me. I don't want to lose him."

Riley shot her a smile. "The only way you would lose Myles is if you told him you didn't love him, and even then, it would take months of him attempting to get you back and you refusing before he thought about giving up. Once a wolf chooses who is his, there's no going back."

"Really?" Addison asked as she sank further into the seat.

Minka leaned up between the two front seats. "Really."

Addison let that knowledge settle into her mind – and her heart. It was almost too much to hope for, to think that she found someone who wouldn't leave her.

"Chiasson blood runs through his veins just as much as LaRue," Riley said as she continued to drive. "It was a Chiasson who left France and settled in Nova Scotia for awhile, bringing his sister and two brothers with him. They eventually made their way down to Louisiana. He settled in Lyons Point while his brothers decided to go different directions to see what the country held."

Addison was transfixed listening to the history of the Chiasson and LaRue families.

Riley smiled as she glanced at Addison and then at Minka. "His sister came to New Orleans with him on a trip and fell in love with a LaRue. She married and taught her husband how to hunt the paranormal."

"I wondered how the LaRues came to be hunters," Minka said as she sat back.

The truck bounced over some deep holes on the dirt road as Riley shrugged. "Being in New Orleans has its perks, but also its drawbacks. Namely, all the beings with some form of supernatural ability."

"I take exception to that," Minka said, but there was no heat in her words.

Addison turned in her seat and said, "Yeah, but you're not trying to kill people. I think Riley is talking about them."

"I am," Riley said. "We have witches in Lyons Point. Hell, Beau is dating one. But I think it's the mix of all the beings in New Orleans that is so different. You see, one of the LaRue children did something to incur the wrath of a Voodoo priestess."

"Oh my God," Minka said with a sigh. "What is it with the LaRues and the priestesses?"

Riley shook her head. "I wish I knew. I don't know what happened to cause the Voodoo priestess to become so angry, but in response, she placed a curse on all LaRues to become werewolves."

Addison turned the water bottle in her hand. "How long will the curse be in place?"

"Forever," Riley and Minka replied in unison.

Addison was outraged. "Are you kidding? That's a little extreme, don't you think?"

"Damn straight," Minka mumbled.

Riley twisted her lips. "My cousins have managed to use it to their advantage. They've befriended witches who have used spells to help them be able to shift whenever they choose instead of only on a full moon. It comes in handy while they hunt in the Quarter."

Minka leaned up again and pointed out the windshield. "There's a live oak with its branches growing on the ground. Take a left there."

Addison peered through the darkness to where the headlights penetrated the night and spotted the gnarly limbs of the large tree having grown so heavy that they did indeed touch the ground.

Riley slowed the truck and turned to the left just as Minka instructed. They rode in silence along the narrow road with thick brush growing up on either side as Myles and the white wolf ran ahead of the truck.

"Damn, girl," Riley said to Minka. "Just how far back in the bayou are we going? This isn't a road. It's a path that hasn't been used in years."

There was silence as Minka remained leaning forward between the two front seats. "It was my great aunt's. She never joined the coven. She didn't trust them or agree with their methods. So she moved off to St. Louis for many years before she returned. She did it without any of the others knowing she was here, and she kept to herself."

"Do the witches get mad if others don't join the coven?" Addison asked.

Minka nodded. "Especially when the coven is made up of family."

Riley and Addison exchanged a quick look.

"My aunt lived out her days on this land in peace," Minka explained. "She left it to me when she died four years ago. I pay someone to keep the place up."

At that moment, the brush cleared and what was left of a white plantation house came into view.

"Please tell me you're not staying there," Addison said when she spotted the second floor porch caving in.

Minka chuckled. "Nope."

"There's nothing else but land and water," Riley said as she slowed the truck to a stop.

Addison followed the beam of the headlights to find Myles watching them. She started to smile, but it slipped when she saw something wet on his shoulder. Her heart missed a beat. "Please tell me that's water and not blood."

"What?" Riley asked as she looked from Addison back outside to Myles. There was a short pause before she said, "It's blood."

"He should've healed already," Minka said. "Unless…"

She trailed off, which made Addison jerked around. "Unless what? What aren't you telling me?"

"Unless silver was used," Riley whispered.

Addison slowly turned back around, but Myles no longer stood in the headlights. "I just found him. I can't lose him."

"Once silver is in their bloodstream, there's no way to stop it. I'm sorry."

"I told him to be careful," Minka said.

Addison squeezed her eyes closed. "You saw his death, didn't you?"

"Yes. I didn't know when it would happen though," Minka added.

Addison opened her eyes. "I'm not going to give up so easily."

She opened the door, ending the conversation. As soon as she did, Myles and the white wolf stood there.

Minka wasted no time in getting out of the truck and walking to Myles. "Idiot. This needs to be seen to."

The white wolf gave a low growl as he noticed the wound. Myles ignored both of them as he stared at Addison. Addison slid from the truck and shut the door. She limped to Myles and touched him while Minka walked to the water.

Riley shut off the engine. "I really hope she's not wanting to go across the bayou."

"Let's find out." Addison winced as she turned and shifted her weight.

The driver's side door shut and Riley came around

the front, her body cutting in front of the headlights that hadn't shut off yet. She looked down at Addison's feet and frowned. "You're not going anywhere."

"I'm not staying here either."

Riley smiled and turned back to open the rear passenger door of the truck. "It's a good thing I always carry extra stuff with me." She dug in the back of the truck for a moment and straightened with another pair of flip-flops. "They're not optimal for trekking in the bayou, but it's better than bare feet."

"Do you always travel with your closet?" Addison asked with a grin.

"I grew up hunting, and I hate to walk around in wet shoes, so I keep extras in my purse."

Addison took a moment to use the light from inside the truck's cabin to clean off her feet and pull out some stickers and a piece of glass. Even with the shoes on, her feet hurt. At least now they were somewhat protected.

"They're going to need to be seen to when we get back to the Quarter," Riley said.

As if to agree, Myles nudged her arm with his cold, wet nose. She smiled and sank her hand into the fur at his neck. She'd seen a wolf at the zoo once, and she knew the werewolves were more than twice their size.

"You should've told me you were hurt," she admonished Myles.

"Oh. Time to go," Riley stated and walked away.

Addison looked to see Minka turn to the left and walk away from the plantation. The white wolf walked beside Minka, and Addison saw two other wolves dart out of the brush and follow them.

She couldn't wait to learn who was who. If she had to guess, Solomon was the white wolf. She knew which one was Myles, and that's all that mattered.

Addison walked as fast as she could with her injured feet to follow Minka and Riley. She was grateful for the shoes when the trail took her through some woods. Myles, limping as well, remained beside her.

All around her were wolves. They made no sounds, but she caught glimpses of them from time to time. With her hand on Myles, she felt safe and comforted. Who knew that could happen with a werewolf.

Addison stepped out of the forest and came to a stop when she saw an old house built on stilts over the bayou, the water gently lapping at the wooden pillars while the moon cast everything in a pale blue glow.

Myles nudged her. She startled and began walking again. Addison eyed the water and the dark shapes she saw.

God, please let this house be in better condition than the plantation. It would be so wrong to be saved from Delphine to die by alligator.

CHAPTER SIXTEEN

Myles was on the porch looking out over the water a half hour after dawn. He and the other wolves had gone into the forest to shift back. He hated leaving Addison, but he wasn't sure she was ready to see all of that quite yet. Not to mention, he wanted a look at his wound first.

Addison slept like the dead after Minka put some salve on her feet and added some herb to her sweet tea. Otherwise, he knew she'd have been right there with him. Myles had remained near, patrolling the porch that went all the way around the small house even as his wound festered.

The wound itself was ugly, black lines branching out as the silver continued to poison him. He had no idea how much longer he had. Every breath was a struggle, but he fought because he wasn't ready to leave Addison.

"Where did you get the clothes?" Minka asked as she came out onto the porch. She sat in one of the wooden chairs and drew her knees up to her chest.

"The truck Riley drove is Kane's. We always keep clothes for such occasions."

"Lucky for you." Minka's smile was soft, sad. "How are you feeling?"

"Like shit," he said. He sighed loudly. "I never saw the blade. I knew Delphine had a bone knife in her hand, but I didn't see a silver one."

Minka dropped her feet to the ground and leaned forward in the chair. "Let me look at it. I might be able to do something."

"You know as well as I that nothing can be done."

"Let her look."

Myles felt his heart plummet to his feet as he heard Addison's voice. He'd remained to see her, but now that she was awake, he knew it would've been better if he'd gone off to die alone.

"Please," Addison said. "Let her try if she can."

Myles couldn't form any words. When Addison came to stand beside him, her arms wrapped around one of his, there wasn't anything she could ask for that he would deny her.

"Am I yours?" she asked.

Myles turned his head to look down into her hazel eyes. "For now and always."

"Then I'll fight for you, just as you fought for me."

He shifted so that he faced her, careful to keep the wound on his left shoulder as hidden as he could. "I don't want to give you false hope."

"It's better than giving up," she replied softly. "Myles, against everything we found each other. I can't explain the attraction or the..." she paused and swallowed loudly. "The love I have for you. I don't want it to end."

As if he would die now without fighting. Myles

touched her cheek. "My sweet Addison. You stole my heart the day you walked into the bar. I desired you, longed for you with such hunger. Then I got a taste of you. I didn't want you in my heart, but you found your way there anyway. Wolves mate for life."

Her eyes were shining with unshed tears. "So I've been told."

"You're mine," he said thickly.

"Then don't leave me."

Minka rose suddenly. "Great. So y'all love each other. Let's get down to business. Addison, go into the kitchen and look in the lower cabinet next to the sink. You'll see a wooden box. Bring it. Myles," she said and pointed to the chair she vacated. "Remove your shirt and sit."

Myles stared after Addison as he did as Minka bade. He ground his teeth together while trying to pull off his shirt. Suddenly, someone gripped the neck of the tee and ripped it in half. He turned and saw Kane beside him.

"This looks like shit," his brother said of the wound.

Myles shrugged his good shoulder. "Feels like it, too."

Boot heels sounded on the porch, and a moment later Solomon and Court were standing in front of him. Myles couldn't hold the gazes of his brothers. He couldn't stand to see the sorrow or anger in their eyes.

Then Addison returned with Minka's box, a small smile on her face that made Myles want to yank her against him and kiss her. It went against everything inside him to waste what little time he had on trying to heal the wound instead of kissing the woman he loved.

"This will work," Addison said with a firm nod.

Myles grinned. "You don't even know what Minka will do."

"Doesn't matter. It'll work."

Minka's look of doubt that she kept hidden from Addison told Myles everything he needed to know. Magic or not, it would be a miracle if Minka were able to reverse the effects of the silver poisoning him.

Kane moved behind Myles, his hands upon his shoulders. Solomon moved to Myles's right while Court walked to the left. There had been a few occasions when wolves tried to stop the silver, and not a single one of them had been painless.

"You should go," Myles told Addison.

She lifted her chin. "Never. I'll be beside you through it all."

"I don't know what will happen," he said, concern about her welfare filling him. "I don't want you hurt."

"She won't be," Griffin said as he and Gage came to stand on either side of Addison.

Myles saw the quick look of interest exchanged between Minka and Griffin, but it was swiftly forgotten when Minka touched his wound. He pulled back his lips as pain ripped through him.

He gripped the handle of the chair but heard the wood crack beneath his hold. Instantly, he felt the hands of his brothers holding him in place even as he squeezed his eyes shut. He thought of Addison, of her tempting mouth and soft body. How unfair to find her only to have to let her go so soon.

Addison couldn't stop the tears no matter how hard she tried. She watched Myles's body shudder in pain as his brothers held him in place. The wound looked horrible, as if his body were rotting from the inside out. And the dark veins spreading outward over his chest and abdomen, down his arm to his hand, and across his back showed how fast the silver spread through him.

Minka, for her part, was working frantically as she searched through herbs applying one after the other to no affect, her face lined with worry.

"Use your magic," Griffin urged her.

Minka cut him a look. "I don't have any."

"Delphine thought differently. Find it, and use it. Or Myles dies."

Myles was shaking from the pain, the black veins growing darker, thicker as the silver moved faster through him. Addison rushed to him, kneeling between his legs. She put her hands atop his.

No one stopped her or tried to push her out of the way. Was it because they knew Myles wasn't going to live? She refused to accept that.

Addison turned her gaze to Minka. "You have magic. Delphine said you did. It's inside you. Please, Minka."

Minka looked from Addison to Myles and then took a deep, shuddering breath. She calmed herself and erased all emotion from her face. Then she placed her hands over Myles's wound and closed her eyes.

Myles jerked, a low growl coming from deep within him. His eyes flew open, glowing yellow as his face contorted with pain. With his teeth beginning to lengthen and his nails growing long and sharp, Griffin tried to drag Addison away.

"No!" she yelled and pulled out of his grasp. "I'm not leaving him."

"Addison!" Solomon yelled over Myles's growls. "He wouldn't want you hurt."

She stood, Myles's gaze locked on her. "I'm not leaving you," she told him and took his face in her hands. Then she leaned down and kissed him.

Myles stilled instantly. When Addison pulled back, his blue eyes had returned. She smiled at him.

"Addison?" he whispered right before he went slack and his eyes shut.

"Myles!" she yelled and shook him.

This time it was Court who took a hold of her and pulled her away. Court held her tightly so there was no way she could get free. She watched as Solomon and Kane backed away with a grim look on their faces.

Addison looked over the porch to see dozens of people – werewolves – watching Myles in silence. She wiped at the tears and noticed Riley for the first time standing just inside the house with her arms wrapped around herself crying silently, her shoulders shaking.

"No," Addison whispered. "I can't lose him. I've lost everyone else."

Griffin placed a hand on her shoulder. "Shh."

She frowned at him but saw that his gaze was on Minka. Addison swiveled her head to the witch. Minka was hovering a few inches off the porch, a strange light surrounding her. Solomon started toward Minka, but Griffin moved with lightning speed, stopping Solomon with a hand on his arm.

"Leave her," Griffin said in a low, dangerous voice.

Solomon's gaze narrowed, his lips pulled back in a snarl. "Why?"

"Because her magic is being released. Look at your brother's wound if you don't believe me."

Addison gasped when she saw the black veins on Myles begin to shrink in size and length until there was nothing but the ugly, festering wound. And then, even that began to heal.

"Impossible," Court murmured.

Griffin was smiling as he said, "No, just not something any witch can do."

Blood began to run from Minka's ears and her nose as the last bit of Myles's injury vanished, ending with a drop of silver that disappeared, as well. Minka went lax but was caught in Solomon's arms before she could hit the floor.

Solomon stared down at her a moment before he gently lifted her and slowly walked her into the house past Riley. Addison shoved Court's hands away and rushed to Myles, but he wasn't moving. Kane and Court quickly lifted him and brought him to the couch inside.

As soon as he was laid down, Addison sat on the floor beside the couch, his hand in hers. She rested her forehead on his side and simply held him, praying that he woke.

~ ~ ~

It was dark when Myles opened his eyes. He grinned when he saw Addison asleep as she leaned against the couch. Myles was careful as he sat up, expecting pain, and when there was none, he looked at his shoulder to find that he was healed. There was a large scar, but no wound.

He gently gathered Addison in his arms and moved her to the couch. As he stood, he saw Minka and Griffin on the porch talking in low voices. The interest in Griffin's eyes was obvious, and Myles suspected Minka might be interested, as well.

Myles was about to walk onto the porch when he caught sight of Solomon standing in the corner of the kitchen looking out the window at Minka and Griffin.

Suddenly, Solomon's gaze swung to him and he smiled.

"I'll be damned," Solomon whispered.

"Minka's magic worked then?" Myles asked.

Solomon motioned to Myles's shoulder. "Obviously. Addison hasn't left your side, or eaten, all day."

Myles would see that changed as soon as she woke. "Where are Court and Kane?"

"With the Moonstone pack."

There was something in the way Solomon said the words, paired with the glare he shot Griffin, that made Myles wonder what was going on. Then he heard Minka's soft laughter and saw Solomon's brow furrow before he turned away.

"Griffin and his wolves have said they would keep an eye on Minka," Solomon stated.

Myles crossed his arms over his chest. "We owe her a debt. I don't think it should be just the Moonstone pack. I think we owe it to Minka to check on her ourselves."

Solomon shrugged and leaned against the kitchen counter. "I agree."

Myles saw Griffin depart and took the opportunity to talk to Minka. He walked outside, softly closing the screen door behind him. There was no air conditioning in the old house, so the windows and doors remained open to let in any breeze available.

"You look much better," Minka said with a smile when she saw him.

He leaned against of the posts. "Because of you. Thank you, Minka. I owe you a debt I'm not sure I'll ever repay."

"I'm glad it worked."

He watched her profile for a moment as she looked

out over the bayou. "Are you sure this is where you want to stay?"

"My great aunt did it. It'll work as long as my coven thinks I'm dead."

"You still need to eat. You'll have to go into town for supplies."

She faced him and shrugged. "I'll be fine for awhile. There are still those that live on the bayou that my great aunt trusted."

"We'll come to check on you when we can." He scratched at his cheek, longing for a shave. "However, the Moonstone pack have promised to keep an eye on you, too."

Minka glanced inside the door to the couch that Addison slept on. "What about y'all? What happens now? We both know Delphine won't give up. There are plenty of witches around for her to use."

"No," he replied with a weary sigh. "She won't give up, but I'm hoping the other factions saw us working with the witches. That could go a long way in convincing the others to join us in defeating Delphine."

"Watch out for my coven. They can't be trusted."

"Isn't that said of all witches?" he teased.

There was no smile on her face. "And keep a close eye on Addison."

"You don't have to worry." He looked inside, his gaze locking on his woman. "I wasn't looking to find someone, and then she walked into my life. Now, I can't live without her."

"Then don't. You two have something special, something most crave with every fiber of their being." Minka pushed away from the railing. "Now, get in there and let her know you're all right."

Myles chuckled, but took her advice and walked

into the house. He sat on the edge of the couch, marveling at his woman. He lifted a lock of champagne blond hair and twirled it around his finger.

Addison cracked open one eye and saw Myles. She sat up and threw her arms around his neck, hugging him tightly. "You're alive. You're really alive."

He held her firmly. "I'm alive."

"I thought I'd lost you."

"For a moment there, I thought I was gone."

She sniffed and buried her head in his neck. "That was the scariest night of my life."

Myles pulled back and cupped her face in his hands. "Addison, I love you with every ounce of my being, but this is my life. I risk it all every night -"

"I know."

"-to help those that need it. If it's too much-"

"It's not."

"-then I understand. There isn't just the hunting, it's also my family being werewolves. And lest we forget, there's Delphine."

"Are you listening to me?" Addison demanded as he pulled his hands away. "I know it's dangerous. I know this is your life. I know you're a werewolf, and that if we ever have children, they will be, as well. I know there's Delphine, and vampires, witches, djinn,, and demons. I know all of it, and I still remain beside you."

He stared at her for a full minute.

Addison shook her head as she looked up at him. "You saved my life. You saved Minka's life. How many people have you and your family saved, Myles?"

"I don't know," he said with a shrug.

"You bear a curse not of your doing. That in itself is amazing," she said. "But then you go the extra mile and protect the Quarter, at the peril of your own life. I know what's out there now. I'll never look at the Quarter the same again, but knowing you and your brothers are there to protect as many as you can makes me smile."

He was the luckiest bastard to ever walk the earth. Myles kissed her hard and quick. "I'm never letting you out of my sight again."

"Good," she said with a wicked smile. "It's taken you long enough."

"I can be a little slow at times, but I eventually come around."

"Hm," Addison said as she smoothed her hands down his chest. "I think I'd like to see more of your place."

"I can make that happen."

Riley made a noise at the back of her throat. "Yes, please do. You're making all of us sick with this love talk."

Myles looked over and saw all three of his brothers standing behind Riley and Minka. Addison blushed and dropped her head onto Myles's shoulder as everyone laughed.

Today was a good day. The LaRues learned to grasp each one tightly because they never knew when the next might come around.

EPILOGUE

Two weeks later...

Two hours before opening, Addison was laughing as she and Myles came out of the kitchen at Gator Bait. She had moved into Myles's place, and though he asked her every day to marry him, she had yet to say yes. She was going to. She just wanted a little more time with him. Everything had happened so fast, but she had no doubt she was meant to be his.

"So you stole the materials out of Tulane and learned to be an accountant that way?" she asked in disbelief.

Myles set the box of rum on the bar and shrugged. "We'd just bought the bar, and each of us had our jobs. I've always liked numbers, just not school. Plus, I didn't want to put a strain on my brothers by going to college."

"How do you know you're not screwing things up?" she asked as she took a bottle of rum from his hand and climbed the stool to stock it on a shelf.

"I hire a CPA every few years to double check me."

She raised a brow. "So you're that smart."

"He was asked to join Mensa," Solomon shouted from the kitchen.

Addison gaped at him. "Mensa? Seriously? The International High IQ Society?"

Myles shrugged and handed her another two bottles.

"Tell me again why you haven't gone back and gotten your degree?" she asked.

"Not interested. It'd be repeating things."

"Yes, but you'd actually have your degree."

"That's what you're for."

She paused in setting the last bottle in place. Then she slowly looked at him. "What?"

He grabbed her by the waist and swung her to the ground. Keeping his hands on her, Myles brought her against him. "You've got one year left. Let me help you finish. We can do the accounting together."

It was in her nature to refuse any handouts, and yet this wasn't a handout. This was from the man she loved, the man she would spend the rest of her life with. How could she refuse him?

"Don't answer now," he said when she hesitated. "Think it over."

Addison rose up on her toes and kissed him. "I love you, Myles LaRue."

"And I love you, Addison Moore, though that should be Addison LaRue."

She laughed as they kissed again. They were interrupted by a throat clearing.

Addison turned her head to see a man with dark hair and bright blue eyes. She didn't need to be told this was a Chiasson. She could see the resemblance between him and Riley.

"Myles," the man said with a smile.

Myles was smiling, his head cocked to the side. "Well, I'll be damned. If it isn't Beau Chiasson."

The two met at the end of the bar and clapped each other on the back in a quick embrace. Addison saw the way Beau looked around and how Myles watched him.

"What brings you to town?" Myles asked.

Beau started to answer when he turned his head toward the kitchen and saw Solomon, Court, and Kane walking out.

Addison walked to Myles and linked her hand with his. In her weeks at Gator Bait, she had come to value Riley's friendship. Riley was still finding her way, and Addison didn't intend to let any of Riley's family – including the LaRues – force Riley to return to Texas.

"Riley," Beau finally answered. "I've come for Riley."

Kane crossed his arms over his chest. "Why do you think she'd come here?"

"Where else would she go?" Beau answered with a crooked smile. "Look, I just want to know she's all right. Vin is losing his mind, and Linc is ready to start scouring Louisiana for her. Christian is in Austin hoping that's where she's at, but I know Riley the best. She was hurt."

"Damn straight I was," Riley said as she came out of the back.

Beau let out a relieved sigh. "Thank God you're all right."

"I'm not going back," Riley stated.

Beau held up his hands. "I'm not here to make you. I intended to, but Davena set my ass straight quick enough. We did you wrong, Riley. Vin isn't ready to admit that, but it's the truth. Take whatever time you need before you return to Texas."

Riley rolled her eyes. "Did you not hear me? I'm not going back. I've no need to return to Texas, dumbass. I've already graduated!"

Addison had to turn away to keep from laughing at Beau's dumbfounded expression.

"You really fucked up there, cuz," Court told Beau.

Beau ignored him and walked to Riley. He pulled her into his arms and hugged her. "I'm sorry, sis. Let me make it up to you?"

"How?" she asked.

"I won't tell them I found you. Call tomorrow and let Vin know things are fine."

Riley was shaking her head before he finished. "No, Vin and Linc will look for me."

"You have my word they won't. Olivia is still angry with Vin, and she won't let him force you to do anything. As for Lincoln, he's not about to do anything to upset Ava again."

Riley stared at him a moment before she sniffed and discreetly wiped at her eyes. "Since you're here, you might as well stay and eat. Where is Davena? I wanted to meet her?"

"She wasn't ready to come to New Orleans just yet after her last run in with Delphine," Beau said as he took a stool at the bar.

Myles glanced at Addison. "She should get ready to do so."

Beau's eyes hardened. "What's happened?"

The rest of the LaRues sat around Beau and began to recount everything. Addison watched it all with interest. If she was going to be a LaRue, it meant the Chiassons were also part of her family.

"What are you smiling at?" Myles whispered in her ear.

"The fact that I've gone from an only child to having an entire family."

Myles turned to look at her. "Are you saying what I think you're saying?"

"Yes," she said with a smile.

Myles let out a whoop and gathered Addison in his arms. "We're getting married!" he shouted.

The two were swarmed by Riley, Solomon, Court, Kane, and Beau congratulating them. Addison couldn't take her eyes from Myles. He was her best friend, her lover, her soon-to-be husband, and her werewolf.

Life couldn't get any better.

Look for the next story in the Chiasson/LaRue series with **MOON THRALL** – Coming **February 9, 2015**!

Until then, read on for the sneak peek at **HOT BLOODED**, the fourth book in the Dark King series out **December 30, 2014**…

Dreagan Industries
June

Laith leaned back in the chair with his hands behind his head as he looked around Constantine's office. There were only a handful of Dragon Kings in the large room. Some were on various missions regarding the Dark Fae, Ulrik, and others that only Con knew about.

Still other Kings were on the sixty thousand acres of Dreagan property tending to livestock, overseeing their famous Dreagan whisky, and patrolling their borders. Because even though their dragon magic kept most humans and other beings out, some still tried to gain entrance.

As a race of shape-shifting immortals who had been around since the dawn of time, the Dragon Kings weren't without their share of enemies. And the list kept growing as the months went by.

Each King was powerful in his own right or he would never have been chosen to rule his dragons, but there was one who was King of Kings—Constantine.

Con with his surfer boy golden blond hair and soulless black eyes could be a cold son of a bitch. He did what was necessary, regardless of who was hurt, in order to keep the secret of Dreagan from leaking to the humans.

While turning the gold dragon-head cuff links at his wrist, Con sat patiently behind his desk staring at a file folder while everyone took their seats.

"What's up?" Ryder leaned over to whisper before promptly taking a bite of a jelly-filled donut.

Laith shrugged. It could be anything, and he learned long ago not to try and guess what was going on in Con's head or try to figure out Con's thinking when he did something. The fact Con wouldn't look up from the folder meant that whatever was inside was troubling indeed.

Kellan was the last to enter Con's office. After a quick look around, Kellan closed the door behind him. The Keeper of the History remained as he was, leaning against the door instead of taking a chair.

Another sign that something bad had happened. Laith took a deep breath and slowly let it out. Besides Ryder, Con, and Kellan there was Rhys, Warrick, Hal, and Tristan. Everyone looked at ease. Except for Rhys.

There was something going on with his friend, but so far Rhys hadn't shared it with anyone. The lines of strain around Rhys's mouth said that whatever bothered him was taking a hard toll.

Rhys ran a hand through his long dark hair, his gaze meeting Laith's. A heartbeat later, Rhys's gaze skated away. Laith scratched his chin, the two-day's growth of beard itching, as he considered how hard to push to get Rhys to tell him—or someone—what was wrong.

"Come on, Con," Tristan said as he bent a leg to set his ankle atop his knee. "Stop stalling. Why did you call us in here?"

Con's black eyes slowly lifted to meet Tristan's. He let the silence lengthen before Con leaned forward and stabbed a finger on the file folder. "This."

"And what is that?" Hal's voice was calm, but as one of six Kings who had taken mates, he was anything but. His gaze was riveted on Con, his bearing anxious and worried.

Con sighed and got to his feet. He shoved his hands in the pockets of his navy slacks. "I'd hoped we would have a reprieve. I'd hoped that Kiril and Shara would have more time to themselves being newly mated."

"For the love of all that's holy, spit it out," Ryder stated, unable to wait any longer.

A muscle in Con's jaw jumped. "John Campbell was found dead this morning."

Everyone stilled, their faces expressing shock, surprise, and disbelief as Con's words penetrated. No one said a word as they comprehended what John's death meant to Dreagan.

Laith closed his eyes, feeling remorse for John's death. The Campbells had owned the fifty acres bordering Dreagan for countless generations. It began shortly after the war with the humans, once the Kings sent the dragons to another realm. There was a doorway onto Dreagan, it was hidden, but could be used by their enemies. Since no Dragon King's magic could touch the area around the doorway, it became apparent that they would have to trust a human to do it for them.

The Campbells, one of the few groups of humans who didn't wage war on Dreagan stepped forward. And so the watch of the Campbells had begun.

Only the head of the family, the one responsible for ensuring no one accidentally stumbled upon the doorway, knew the secret of Dreagan and what it was being guarded. It continued in that vein for thousands of years through wars and invasions. The Campbells kept the Dragon Kings' secret, and the Kings, in turn, protected them.

How Laith was going to miss John's laughter and his jokes. John hadn't just protected Dreagan, he'd become a friend.

"Who's going to guard the land?" Laith asked.

Kellan glanced at Con. "John has a daughter, Iona."

"That's right. I forgot about her," Rhys said.

Hal frowned as he sat forward and rested his arms on his legs. "She's been gone for a while, aye?"

"A verra long while," Con said. "Twenty years in fact."

Laith shifted to get comfortable in the chair. "John often talked of Iona. He showed me her photographs when he'd come into the pub. For as long as I knew him, and as often as we chatted, he never told me what happened with his wife."

Con stood and walked behind his tall chair, leaning his arms upon the back. "One of John's responsibilities was to remain on the land."

"He remained when his wife left and took Iona," Hal said softly.

Laith shifted his gaze back to Con. "He could've left for that."

"He took his oath to us seriously," Kellan explained. "To help with the pain of his loss, he buried himself in his writing after that."

Warrick nodded slowly. "He was an excellent writer."

"That he was." Con looked at the file folder again.

Laith dropped his arms to his lap. "What's in the

file, Con? If it was only a matter of ensuring his daughter take up her father's duties, we wouldna been called here."

"Iona stepping into her duties is another matter entirely. I'll get to that in a moment. What's in the folder is a report. John didna die by natural causes," Con said as he locked his gaze on Laith's. "He was murdered."

Thank you for reading **Moon Kissed**. I hope you enjoyed it! If you liked this book – or any of my other releases – please consider rating the book at the online retailer of your choice. Your ratings and reviews help other readers find new favorites, and of course there is no better or more appreciated support for an author than word of mouth recommendations from happy readers. Thanks again for your interest in my books!

Donna Grant

www.DonnaGrant.com

Want to stay informed of new releases and special subscriber-only exclusive content?

Be sure to visit

www.DonnaGrant.com

and sign up for Donna's private email newsletter!

ABOUT THE AUTHOR

New York Times and *USA Today* bestselling author Donna Grant has been praised for her "totally addictive" and "unique and sensual" stories. She's written more than thirty novels spanning multiple genres of romance including the bestselling Dark King series featuring immortal Highlander shape shifting dragons who are daring, untamed, and seductive. She lives with her husband, two children, a dog, and four cats in Texas.

Connect online at:

www.DonnaGrant.com

www.facebook.com/AuthorDonnaGrant

www.twitter.com/donna_grant

www.goodreads.com/donna_grant/

Printed in Great Britain
by Amazon